THE SIGN OF THE FOX

THE SIGN OF THE FOX

A NOVEL

SARA STAMBAUGH

Good Books
Intercourse, PA

Acknowledgments

Design by Dawn J. Ranck

Cover design by Cheryl A. Benner

THE SIGN OF THE FOX
© 1991 by Good Books, Intercourse, PA 17534
International Standard Book Number: 1-56148-011-8
Library of Congress Catalog Card Number: 91-70665

Library of Congress Cataloging-in-Publication Data

Stambaugh, Sara, 1936-
  The Sign of the Fox / Sara Stambaugh.
     p.   cm.
  ISBN 1-56148-011-8 : $16.95
     1. Pennsylvania—History—1775–1865—Fiction.   I. Title.
PS3569.T3312S57   1991
813′ .54—dc20   91-70665
                                                          CIP

To Jack and Nancy

To Jack and Nancy

Preface

Although, as always, I have drawn from memories of home, the plot and characters in this book are imaginary. For the historical context I owe special thanks to friends I made through the libraries of the Lancaster Historical Society and the Lancaster Mennonite Historical Society and, especially, to the staffs of both. The University of Alberta kindly gave me time to write and assistance in preparing the manuscript. Not surprisingly, my biggest debts are to my family and friends from Lancaster and from Kitchener, Ontario, as well as to *The New Quarterly* which published an early draft of the opening chapters.

Preface

1.

In the fall of 1828 the nation was still being built. Southeastern Pennsylvania had been settled for a hundred years, long enough for the farm people to absorb its rhythms, though the Mennonites of Lancaster County were still dragging rocks from fields and only beginning to build houses fit to stand beside their great, cathedral-like barns.

But William Penn's Holy Experiment opened his colony to people of all persuasions, not just Quakers and other pacifists. If Mennonite farmers minded the land, the English and Scots Irish looked after the government, as some German families did as well, joining the Presbyterian church, anglicizing their names, and scrambling after business.

The Carpenters had been Zimmermans when they came to the new world, where they soon made their house a substantial one. Having carefully distanced themselves from their German neighbors, they were now the proprietors of a thriving inn. Clearly, the Carpenters were upper-class, in spite of any twaddle about equality from that firebrand, Andrew Jackson.

At the Sign of the Fox, the family was consulting in the upstairs parlor reserved for family and people of quality, like the gentleman sitting with his chair tilted against the chairboard. Everyone in the neighborhood knew that Will and Penelope Carpenter were having a morning visit from their son Sam, who'd left his law practice to ride the three miles from Lancaster in response to a message from his father.

Will Carpenter leaned forward. "I tell you," he barked, shaking a letter, "this news from your Aunt Sophie is enough to ruin the family!" The Squire glared at his son, daring him to contradict.

Sam waited, knowing better than to answer before his mother had her say, while his sister Martha silently turned the heel on the stocking she was knitting.

"Samuel," Penelope Carpenter pronounced to her son, "we're counting on you to talk your sister out of this latest harebrained notion of hers. Heaven knows, Eleanor is flighty enough that I gave up trying to reason with her years ago."

"That maybe is the root of the problem," the Squire growled.

His wife adjusted her shawl, looked at him imperiously, and repeated, "I gave up trying years ago." Her authority re-established, the mistress of the Fox went on, "The difference this time is that she's gotten Sophie to speak up for her. Imagine, my own sister telling us that Eleanor has to come home!" She sniffed and added for her husband's benefit, "And if your daughter is flighty, Mr. Carpenter, you can't say the same thing for my sister Sophie."

Sam didn't seem surprised, perhaps because he'd expected the problem, perhaps because like any other lawyer, he'd learned to look as though he had. He fingered his sideburns, which his mother saw as another signal of her son's aristocracy. Samuel took after her people, the Passmores, she often pointedly remarked to Martha, who had unfortunately inherited her father's square face along with more than a touch of his shrewdness—which no one ever noticed, thanks to her more interesting brother and sister.

Rocking his chair with either nonchalance or impatience, Sam asked precisely what his Aunt Sophie had written, and the Squire thrust out the letter.

While Sam read it, his mother dabbed her eyes with a lace-edged handkerchief. "When I think of all the fuss and trouble we had with that girl," she blurted between dabs, "and how, with all her chances, she wouldn't think of having anyone but Alexander Johns! Sensitive, she said he was, and artistic — as if any sane person had time for that kind of nonsense!"

Mrs. Carpenter herself had little time for nonsense, and being a lady didn't keep her from running the Fox, even though the inn wasn't a stage tavern any more, as it used to be in her father-in-law's day, before the Lancaster-Philadelphia Turnpike a mile south drew away fast traffic and left the Old Philadelphia Road a freight route. Local stages and gentlemen travellers still stopped, but most of the Fox's business nowadays was downstairs in the taproom.

Penelope Passmore Carpenter had clear ideas about her relationship to the downstairs customers, too. She served them if she had to with suitable loftiness, but that business was ordinarily taken care of by the bonded help or whatever hired girls she could find. Still, she worked constantly, leisure and similar nonsense being privileges reserved for children who took after the Passmore side of the family.

"It seems to me, Mama, you were happy enough when she set her cap on him," grumbled her husband, conveniently forgetting his own pride over Eleanor's marriage, since the Johns family controlled the stage line between Newport and Columbia, and were a major power in the eastern end of the county.

"Just to think," Mrs. Carpenter wailed, ignoring him, "married three years, and now Eleanor wants to leave her husband!"

Without a pause in her knitting, Martha commented, "I never heard of a wife leaving her husband." Surprisingly, her father took up her remark.

"Of course you ain't!" he exploded. "No decent woman leaves her man! Why, if that sort of thing went on, it would kick the world clean out of its traces!" He glared at his unmarried daughter as if he held her personally responsible.

By now Sam had finished the letter. "Aunt Sophie says more about butchering and candlemaking than about this business with Eleanor," he commented noncommittally, handing the letter back to his father.

"I didn't fetch you from Lancaster for mealymouthed law talk," the Squire retorted. "You can save that for them as pay you for it and tell your own family what you make of this. Sophie says Eleanor ain't staying with Alec and is coming home, and I'm asking you, what are we going to do about it?"

Knitting steadily, Martha studied her brother's face. "Aunt Sophie's been with Eleanor more than a month now," she remarked. The others ignored her.

"You can count on it, there's more to this than Aunt Sophie's put on paper," Sam said after a pause. "She's been there long enough to see how the land lies, and she and Eleanor always were close."

"We all know that," growled the Squire, intimidated by his son and never sure he wasn't being baited (one of the inconveniences of having a son with a fancy education). "Now we'll thank you for your advice — if you have any to spare for your own family." All three looked at Sam.

Sam fingered his sideburns. "In that case," he said slowly, "the only thing we can do is — nothing." Before his father could interject, he leaned forward. "Aunt Sophie says Eleanor is coming home, and that's that. There's nothing strange about a woman visiting her family, and no one has to know there's any more to it. Once she's here, we'll have time to find out why she left and arrange whatever has to be done."

"Or ship her back to the man she belongs to," the Squire muttered.

Sam shook his head. "With Eleanor, it's never that easy. We'll know how serious all this is if she brings the piano," he added, pulling a watch from his pocket and checking it against a grandfather clock currently showing a profile of the moon above the dial. Sam shook his head at the discrepancy with his watch and stood up. Having clients to meet, he advised his parents to act as if Eleanor were making an ordinary visit, promising as he pulled on his coat to come back Sunday, after Eleanor got in from Christiana — with or without her piano.

The minute he was gone, Martha put away her knitting and went to look after the upstairs cleaning, while husband and wife made their way downstairs to the kitchen and taproom. Sam left by a set of outside steps leading to the back of the inn, where Gumbo Jim, his father's bonded slave, fetched his horse from the stable. Soon the family legal expert was cantering back to Lancaster.

From the north the Sign of the Fox seemed to face the Old Road, because of the doors and long porch over what looked like the ground floor of a large stone house, shingled with slate and topped with four chimneys. But beside the sign near its eastern end, a lane led down an incline to the south side, where it opened into a courtyard, thick with mud from the November rains. South of it were outbuildings, including a two-and-a-half story spring house flanked by a bake oven, a stable, and a carriage shed. Beside the shed was a lean-to where a chained eagle huddled under a makeshift roof. A barn stood across the lane.

But as the view from the courtyard showed, the Fox, like many German buildings, was set into a hill and really faced south. Its foundation was the ground story, out of sight from the road and built up by successive owners to a height, from this side, of three and a half stories.

The real entrance to the Fox was here, past a hitching rail, a stone block to help ladies dismount, a wooden pump, and a pair of footscrapers. One door led to the taproom and another to the kitchen, while the steps Sam had used took gentlemen and ladies directly to the more exalted rooms upstairs.

Squire Carpenter ruled the taproom. Low-ceilinged and

small, the room accommodated a surprising number of activities, besides the ones provided from kegs. A table near the tapster's grate held newspapers, some in English and some in German, dropped off by stage and waiting to be read by local farmers, while a desk on one end of the table showed that more business went on here than tallying pints and quarts. Like other prosperous and respected innkeepers, Squire Carpenter was banker for many of his neighbors and often looked after their legal affairs (even though he transacted more serious business and his work as justice of the peace in his office upstairs). The Squire also kept a good house, with sharp cider and pungent rum flip. And snooty as she was, Mrs. Carpenter laid a good board upstairs and had leftovers for anyone below who called for food with his ale and wanted more than a sup or two of what the tapster had to offer.

Laying the board wasn't always easy, however, and Mrs. Carpenter was in a constant state of crisis over the cooks, who succeeded one another with alarming regularity. The inn was generally well staffed, thanks to hired help and especially Gumbo Jim the hostler, a pauper boy, and a family of German redemptioners in one of the tenant houses, whom the Squire had purchased in various transactions. One by one, the bonded help would work out their time, though not for several years more. But though the German redemptioner minded the tapster's grate, not one of the others could be trusted with the cooking.

While the Squire went to the taproom to greet customers in for a morning dram, Mrs. Carpenter inspected the kitchen. Two fires were burning in the fireplace, which all but filled the east end of the room. A kettle bubbled over one and a spit hung over the other, but the roast of pork dangling over it was remarkably black and the fire particularly orange and fierce, spitting up more smoke with each new drip of fat. As Mrs. Carpenter arrived, flames shot up, enveloping the main course for the day. "Patience!" Mrs. Carpenter screamed.

A slatternly woman burst through the door, snatched up a

pitcher, and dashed it over meat and fire, raising a cloud of steam—and a strong smell of alcohol.

White with anger, Mrs. Carpenter surveyed the perpetrator of the most recent cooking disaster. By now, Patience Slack had grabbed a broom and was stabbing it into the fireplace, trying to keep the second fire from going out. As it, too, sizzled and died, the woman looked up. "It ain't like I can do everything at onct, Missus!"

"No," pronounced Mrs. Carpenter, biting off her words. "It doesn't look as if you can do anything at all. How dared you to tell me you could cook, when you can't even mind a fire?"

Patience Slack glared at her employer. "Maybe I can, too," she retorted, "when I ain't fetching my own water and drawing beer and cider for them in the next room, what with nobody else to look to it half the time!"

Mrs. Carpenter picked up the empty jug from the table where her cook had thumped it down. One sniff was enough. "You seem to have plenty of time to serve yourself," the Squire's wife said icily.

"And why not, I'd like to know?" flared back the cook, wiping her hands on her apron and tucking some straggling hair under her cap. "How else am I supposed to make up for the wages you don't pay me? It ain't like I live here and work myself sick out of charity to you and the mister."

With restraint worthy of the Passmores, Mrs. Carpenter said acidly, "Is that all?"

"No, it ain't, either," shot back the cook. "I ain't stayin' here no longer unless you start payin' me right. Why, any time I want, I can walk down the road to Enterprise and get better than a dollar and a quarter a week at the Bird-in-Hand!"

Mrs. Carpenter snorted with indignation. "Perhaps you should think about doing just that," she pronounced. "I'll expect you and your traps out of the Fox on Saturday. Right now," she added, "—if you can spare the time—you'll oblige me by fetching coals and getting these fires going!"

2.

A few hundred yards east of the Fox a road turned off to the north and meandered through fields, meadows, and woods until it eventually joined the New Holland Pike. Scattered along the road were farms, some built of log and thatched with rye straw, others of stone, and some here and there of brick, with wood, slate, or tile shingles.

A cluster of farm buildings three-quarters of a mile up the road was typical. The stone barn was flanked by neat outbuildings, while near it, incongruously, stood a log house. Still, it appeared that soon the family it belonged to planned on living as well as their cattle, because a hole gaped beside the dwelling, obviously prepared for the stone house starting to rise above it.

Like most Mennonites, Gideon Landis believed in putting first things first, and economic realities necessarily came before creature comforts. But after several years of good crops and the sale of some land, he'd finally given in to his wife's promptings and, crops harvested and disposed of, was building the house she wanted. A mason had been hired and stone hauled from the quarry next to the thirty-five acres which had, in effect, been exchanged for the new house—and comfort at last for Elizabeth.

On this overcast and chilly afternoon, Gideon was following someone else's orders for a change, fetching stones and mixing mortar for the mason, while fifteen-year-old Peter handed up whatever trowel, chisel, or plumb line Mr. Rees needed from one stone to the next.

All three looked up from their work as a spring wagon clattered down the road and into the lane, driven by a fat man with a red face and cheeks like balloons on either side of his sharp nose. The visitor pulled up his horse and sat looking on, till Gideon put down the stone he was carrying and walked over.

"Sure is good to see folks working," the visitor said jovially.

Gideon smiled, knowing full well that his neighbor liked watching better than doing. John Skiles lived a mile and a half farther down the road and never missed a chance to put off going home by a stop at the Fox and visits along the way, so that even hauling grain to the mill could take up the better part of his day. Still, as a result, Skiles was the unofficial news center for this part of the Conestoga Valley, always first with word of births, deaths, and ailments, not to mention politics, a subject always dear to his heart but especially now, with presidential elections only a few weeks off. Gideon wasn't surprised when Skiles's opening topic was the contest between Adams and Jackson, Skiles slyly asking whether Gideon had amalgamated yet and joined the new party supporting Jackson.

Gideon shook his head, and Skiles pretended to be surprised. "It wonders me you still ain't ready to throw that fancypants New Englander out and put in a common man like you and me," he said, clicking his tongue. As seriously as his fat cheeks would let him, he poked his nose at Gideon and added, "It ain't right, sitting back and letting them as thinks they're better than the rest of us run the country. Why, if things don't change, this here ain't going to be no kind of a democracy."

Gideon shrugged. "Now Chon," he answered in a German accent, "we've been neighbors long enough, you know I can't support a man that lived in sin for years and killed his fellow men in cold blood. A man like Adams at least got the education to run things, and I can't see how Jackson's going to do any better."

Since Landis's political stance was too firm to be swayed, Skiles shifted to new ground, prying into every detail of the new house. As he went on to ask about Elizabeth's health, Gideon smiled to himself, knowing full well that Skiles cared less whether his wife was over her summer fever than whether she was expecting another child.

In answer, Gideon described her toothache the week before, when Elizabeth's face swelled so big, he said Skiles would have thought she was his own sister.

Skiles half suspected that Gideon was pulling his leg, but he never could tell. He respected Landis enough that he'd watched what he did to his fields ever since Gideon moved here from across the Susquehanna twelve years ago. But except for his skill in farming, Skiles thought something must be loose in Gideon's upper story, especially after the time he'd come over to borrow oats and asked Landis to lend him a bucket. "No trouble," Gideon had answered, and handed him an empty one, asking soberly, "Will this one do?" For perhaps the twentieth time, Skiles decided that, at the least, his neighbor had trouble understanding English.

His own questions stopped and Gideon pointedly looking at the boy and man working on the house, Skiles got down to passing on the serious news: which young people were courting and the fight Mrs. Carpenter just had with her latest cook. Saving the best till last, he asked, "You hear about Miles Wilson?"

Gideon looked at him sharply, because it was Miles Wilson who'd bought the thirty-five acres next to the quarry. Wilson had paid earnest money, but Gideon agreed to wait for the rest till New Year's. He'd hired the mason on the strength of that agreement, knowing that if the house wasn't started while farm work was slack, Elizabeth would wait another year for it. And, as she pointed out, their daughter Catherine was old enough that by now they needed a parlor.

Savoring the weight of his news, Skiles pronounced, "Died yesterday. It was all the talk at the Fox this forenoon. I heard tell he had two strokes—only the second one took him." He went on to describe how Wilson's wife found him and put him to bed, where he'd rallied enough to ask for beef and bread-and-butter pickles. "He hadn't half et his plate, Margie said, when it come on him, and next thing she knew, his face was purple, and he was stone dead—I never did think Margie was much of a cook," he added disapprovingly.

Gideon was more shaken than he cared to show, not just because a man two years younger than he was had been cut down, but because, he realized, with Wilson dead he couldn't count on the money to pay Owen Rees, the mason. After a pause, he said slowly, "May the Lord be with him." He didn't mention his personal concern, knowing that if he did, it would be all over the township in twenty-four hours, and Gideon Landis didn't think his affairs were the business of all Lampeter.

But Skiles must have picked up word of them at the Fox, too, because he asked briskly, "Wilson pay you for that thirty-five acres yet?"

Gideon shook his head, and Skiles leaned over confidentially. "If I was you," he said, "I'd take me a little trip to the Fox and see the Squire, onct. He's executin' Miles's will." News delivered, Skiles was soon clattering out the lane, savoring what he'd picked up to pass on at his next stop along the way.

For once, Gideon took his neighbor's advice, but not till after he'd put in a day's work and finished supper. It wasn't unusual for Mennonites to visit taverns. In fact, farm breakfasts were often washed down with small beer or cider, and farm women regularly made wine (for medicinal purposes), just as their husbands regularly turned grain into whiskey at one or the other of the distilleries dotting the countryside, many owned by fellow Mennonites.

Inns were respectable enough, though some of them were clearly more respectable than others, the reason Gideon avoided the Drover, half a mile east of the Fox. It catered to itinerants driving herds of cattle and pigs from the West, and the men who visited its taproom were likely to be none of the best. The Fox, on the other hand, was a place to read the papers or carry out business with the help of the Squire, whose father before him had looked after the welfare of the countryside.

It was well after dark when Gideon got back from consulting with the Squire. Short as days were in the waning of the year, his family was still up and gathered around the fireplace, built where it could warm the bedroom behind it, while it heated and lighted the main room. Kitchen, dining room, and sitting room in one, the room showed why Elizabeth needed a bigger house for herself and her children.

Everyone was busy. Peter was picking meats from a basin of cracked walnuts and helping his little brothers as they puzzled over an English ABC, while Elizabeth sat at the end of the table sewing. Catherine, Gideon's eighteen-year-old daughter, was twisting thread at a tall spinning wheel, her blond hair gleaming in the firelight.

Elizabeth looked up and greeted him in German, her face warm and pretty in spite of her recent illness. Like the rest of the family, she was dressed conservatively but not very differently than her neighbors. She wore a cape, the points tucked in at her waist, and a cap with fluting on the band which framed her face attractively. Seeing her at work in the cramped room, Gideon thought to himself for perhaps the tenth time, that if the Lord meted out according to worth, Elizabeth deserved a proper house.

As he hung his hat and coat on a peg by the door, Elizabeth cheerfully asked whom he'd run into at the Fox. Gideon gave a general answer and rummaged after some harness that needed mending. The boys were talking among themselves, Catherine occasionally leaving her spinning to peer over their shoulders and offer advice when their book included a phrase beyond Peter's skill in English.

Harness and tools in hand, Gideon sat down at the table next to Elizabeth. "I went to see the Squire," he said. Surprised to hear him speaking English, Elizabeth glanced at him inquiringly. Catherine and Peter were fluent in English, but Gideon's use of it signalled that what he had to say was best kept from the little boys, who at six and ten didn't know much of the language.

Over supper Gideon hadn't mentioned Wilson's death, preferring to wait till he'd learned how it might affect his affairs. Now he announced it to his wife, adding, "The upshot is, we won't get paid till the will's settled, and the Squire says that may take a spell, a couple months, anyhow."

Still weak from her summer ague, Elizabeth started to cough. The children stopped reading, and Peter was listening intently. Catherine, too, hurried to her mother's side to help her if she needed to, and to hear better. The children didn't know much about Gideon's affairs, but the family had talked regularly about the new house, and all four knew that it had finally been started because Wilson had bought their father's land.

"Can't we finish the house now?" asked Peter.

"It's worse than that, goosie," Catherine said, putting her hand on her mother's shoulder.

By now Elizabeth had recovered from her coughing fit. She pushed away her sewing and studied Gideon's face. "If he can't pay us, how are we going to pay Owen Rees?" she asked.

Gideon shook his head. "When I took him on, we bargained I'd give him the lump in January, after he finished the walls," he said. "All I can do now is tell him what happened and ask him to wait."

"And if he don't want to?" Elizabeth asked, adding quietly, "We're obliged for what's bargained."

"We'll have to raise the money somehow," Gideon answered. "For now, all I can see is taking on any extra work I can find."

Elizabeth's needle resumed its course, but her mouth twitched. At the end of the table the little boys, bored at a conversation they couldn't understand, were reciting alphabet rhymes. "A dog will bite/A thief at night," Paul intoned.

"Hush up now," Gideon said sharply. Round-eyed, Benny and Paul looked at their father, then went back to their book, studying it quietly now, except for occasional exaggerated whispers.

"It's a pity they haven't started that railroad they're talking on yet," Elizabeth remarked. "Then there'd be work enough. Have you thought of anyone that might take you on?"

Gideon shrugged. "Adam Wenger's not as spry as he used to be and wants help wagonmaking." He added, "But I couldn't start till the walls are up. I bargained with Rees to help him do the job, and I can't take back my word halfway through."

Elizabeth nodded, agreeing that Gideon couldn't go back on a promise.

"I heard some other news, though," Gideon said, his mouth relaxing and his eyes twinkling. Peter, Catherine, and Elizabeth expected more jokes on John Skiles, whom they'd seen stopping. Instead, Gideon said, "Patience Slack, down at the Fox, finally got to be too much for Mrs. Carpenter and got her comeuppance. They had a nice set-to this morning. The upshot is, the Slack woman got thrown out, lock, stock, and barrel."

In spite of herself, Elizabeth smiled. Patience Slack had a reputation as a ne're-do-well, and from the time she started cooking at the Fox, people in the neighborhood had speculated how long she'd last. Catherine, who had returned to her spinning, and Peter, adding to his pile of black walnuts, both laughed, imagining the scene.

Elizabeth looked up. "Now the Fox must want a new cook," she said.

"Now Libby," Gideon said, guessing his wife's thoughts. "You can't take on more work. You have enough to do here."

Elizabeth bent over her needle, knowing full well that Gideon really meant that she wasn't strong enough. She said quietly, "But we can spare Katlie, ain't?"

Catherine was all ears. Mennonite girls often hired out to help towards stocking their hope chests and putting something away towards marriage, though they were most likely to live with another farm family, one with children too young to help with the kitchen work. Only a few worked at public places, but there was no special reason they couldn't, since it gave them the chance to get the worldliness out of their systems before they married and joined church. Working at the Fox would be an adventure, and Catherine would meet more people than she knew from church or weekend frolics.

She was happy enough as she was and hadn't thought of leaving home until now, but at the idea of working at the Fox her eyes sparkled, and she burst out, "Oh, Pap, could I?"

Instead of answering, Gideon spoke to Elizabeth, describing the temptations of working at a public inn. Catherine listened breathlessly and sighed with relief when her father ended his sermon by saying, "Still, like it or not, we haven't got much choice. We'll have to let her go.

"It pays fifty cents a week plus room and board, for starts," he added shortly, "and Mrs. Carpenter says she'll raise it to seventy-five if Katlie proves out."

By now the little boys were squabbling and kicking one another under the table. Rather than disciplining them, Elizabeth quietly told Catherine to put them to bed.

When Catherine climbed back down from the loft, she learned that her father was sending Peter to Adam Wenger's to learn wagonmaking. Peter was exultant, but her mother sat weeping softly, overcome with the shock of losing two of her children. Gideon was talking softly to his wife in German, justifying his decisions and explaining that by mining the quarry by the south field, stopping extra work on the new house, and hoarding the children's earnings, they should be able to pay Owen Rees no later than the spring.

3.

It was Sunday afternoon, the day when, for once, regular customers honored their wives with the pleasure of their company, though the Fox stayed open for travelling ladies and gentlemen. In the morning Mr. and Mrs. Carpenter made a foray into Lancaster to sit in their rented pew in the Presbyterian church, leaving Martha to mind the inn and look after her sister, who had arrived from Christiana Thursday in a flurry of trunks and bandboxes. Sophia Passmore delivered her and drove off shortly after, called away to yet another stricken relative. Eleanor's piano was delivered Friday, to the indignation of the Squire, who ordered the teamsters to set it on the porch.

When the Carpenters got home, accompanied by Sam on his sorrel gelding, Mrs. Carpenter bustled downstairs to instruct the new girl about three o'clock dinner, and the Squire ordered Martha out of the parlor, commenting that he and his son could do without female gabble. Sunday or not, the Squire wasn't one to pass by a consultation with the family legal expert—or word of political developments likely to affect his fortunes, for better or for worse.

Today he wanted to know what Sam had picked up about the railway the State Assembly had authorized the year before and which was now well into planning stages. Surveyors had been wandering the countryside for months, but no decisions were public. So far all anyone knew was that the line was going through Lampeter on its way to Columbia. The question was, precisely where? And more to the point, through whose property?

Never one to beat around the bush, as soon as Martha swished from the room, Will Carpenter demanded the news about it.

"Of course, it's all confidential," Sam answered, studying his fingernails to test his father's patience.

Possibly mellowed by his morning dose of religion, the Squire waited, fingers laced over his paunch and thumbs twiddling with the silver buttons on his waistcoat. Satisfied at his father's patience, Sam said, "I had supper with Nick last night."

The Squire's eyes gleamed, and he leaned forward. "I didn't hear he was back from Harrisburg. What's McMaster picked up on news about the railroad?"

Ignoring the question, Sam remarked, "I ordered in a roast guinea. The two of us sat over our Madeira till after twelve."

The Squire nodded, satisfied that his son's education was a canny investment, well paid by intimacy with an influential assemblyman like Nicholas McMaster, who knew everything affecting his constituency. Besides, McMaster had the governor in his pocket for certain maneuvers critical in the last gubernatorial election.

Still, the Squire's patience was limited. Assured that Sam's news was confidential, he barely stopped himself from ordering him to get on with it. "Well, then?" he asked gruffly.

Suddenly finding a tongue, Sam explained the construction decided on for the railway. Metal rails for the cars and wagons were to rest on wooden beams, those in turn set on stones big enough to give a solid foundation but leaving a horse path in between.

"They can get the wood anywhere," Sam finished, "and the rails have to come from Philadelphia. But believe me, there's money in it for anyone with a quarry near the tracks—if he can get one of the concessions." He smiled at his father and scratched the palm of his hand.

"Seems to me, all that depends on where they put the tracks," growled his father. "Has your friend McMaster picked word up on that?"

"That reminds me, Father," Sam remarked, seemingly at random. "My wine cellar is low. Could you spare a few bottles if I sent Andrew out next week?"

In spite of himself, the Squire smiled. "I'll look for him Tuesday," he said. "How much Madeira did it take, anyhow?"

"Nick likes his drop," Sam replied. "He gave a few hints over the second bottle—not breaking any confidence, you understand, but just to show his appreciation. He said he hadn't tasted any better in two years. Over the third—we started with the Constantia and moved onto the Diploma—he said the tracks were coming due east from the Gap, swinging north near Pequea, and crossing the Old Road east of here at Enterprise. From there they'll run towards Lancaster—just north of the Fox." Cool as he usually was, Sam was clearly exhilarated.

"By the Lord Harry," his father said, with a smile stretching into the folds on either cheek, "that news calls for another drop of Madeira." Telling his son he'd be back in a wink, he pushed himself up and hurried downstairs, while Sam studied the grandfather clock ticking to the steady swing of the pendulum. The quarter moon currently disappearing above the dial smiled slyly, though, as usual, Sam studied the hands. Compulsively, he pulled out his watch.

When the Squire returned with a bottle of his second-best Madeira, Sam said, "I wish you'd let me set that clock and put the time where it belongs."

"My boy," replied the Squire, "I've kept on top of the times by keeping ahead of them, and that's something you can be thankful for, or you'd of done without that fancy education of yours. Half an hour don't make much difference, only it's the principle that counts."

Sam shrugged, as used to his father's answer as his father was to his question. Then, drawing their chairs close to the table with the bottle and glasses, they examined precisely where the tracks for the railroad would run. To the Squire's delight, almost half a mile was sure to cross his land.

Drawing an imaginary map on the table, Sam's finger slowly moved east. "Our property ends here," he said. "Who owns this next piece?"

"The Lord only knows just now," rumbled the Squire. "That would be Gideon Landis's, except for one thing, and that's that a month ago he sold it to Miles Wilson. I guess like everybody else, Landis calculated they'd run the tracks south on the other side of the Pike."

"A bad sale for Landis and a good buy for Wilson," Sam said slowly. "Wilson's a lucky man."

Will Carpenter snorted. "Not so lucky, neither," he said, "seeing as he dropped dead last week." He explained the terms of the sale and his own role as executor of the will, complicated by Wilson having no issue, the bulk of his estate left to six or seven brothers and sisters scattered half across the Union and a life interest to his wife. "A couple of them live in Tennessee," the Squire concluded, "and another one's somewhere out in Kentucky."

Sam sipped his Madeira. "Landis," he pronounced slowly. "Is that the Landis that has a quarry not far from here?"

Will Carpenter held his glass to the light and studied it like a crystal ball. "That's the man," he said, "and that quarry of his is right next to the parcel of land he sold Wilson. We'll have to think some on that," he added meditatively. "The question now is," he added briskly, "what are we going to do about this business with your sister?"

They'd hardly begun to examine that problem when the

clock struck the half hour. Simultaneously, father and son downed their wine, and the Squire pushed himself up from his chair. "We got travellers," he said, "and we can't keep them waiting on their dinner."

The table was set for family and guests alike and loaded with enough food to satisfy twice the number of people sitting there. As the Squire sat down at the head of the table, Mrs. Carpenter took her place near the kitchen stairs, while Martha bustled about arranging last-minute dishes. The guests were three gentlemen and a lady, all impatiently waiting for the Squire's permission to eat. Before he gave it, however, he frowned at an empty chair. "I hope your daughter knows what time it is," he growled to his wife.

"The princess is probably adding a flounce to her dress," Sam remarked, "or arranging an artistic curl." The guests eyed the food. One, a dandified gentleman in a flowered waistcoat, leaned back in his chair and yawned ostentatiously.

Frowning at the empty chair, the Squire raised a glass and said, "Gentlemen, your health." He nodded to the lady traveller. Instantly, serving dishes passed from hand to hand, family and travellers alike bent on filling plates and stomachs as fast as possible. Occasionally, a pretty blond girl appeared at the kitchen stairs to exchange a new platter for an empty one.

Suddenly the clink of cutlery was interrupted. "By Jove!" exclaimed the dandified gentleman, fork midway to his mouth.

"My sister always has liked grand entrances," Sam remarked to no one in particular, while the dandified gentleman (a traveller from England) jumped from his chair. Hurrying to the door and offering his arm, he escorted Eleanor Carpenter Johns to the empty place beside his own.

If Martha looked like her father, Eleanor didn't. Penelope Carpenter was attractive enough for her age, but what was sharp in her was soft in her daughter, who, as Mrs. Carpenter liked to point out, had the Passmores' dark hair and eyes, without a trace of the Carpenters' general redness. Without a doubt, Eleanor Johns was a beauty, and without a doubt she knew it.

As Sam had remarked, Eleanor's entrance was grand enough to rivet everyone's attention. "My younger daughter, Mrs. Johns," Will Carpenter growled to the company.

All the travelling gentlemen stopped eating and simultaneously started passing dishes to the new arrival, while the travelling lady eyed Mrs. Johns critically, looking for faults. However, the sleeves of Mrs. Johns' cherry-colored dress were fashionably puffed at the shoulder, and for jewelry she wore only an elegant pearl locket. The travelling lady stared at the mole on Eleanor's left cheek. But when Mrs. Johns laughingly protested at the food the dandified gentleman was piling on her plate and showed that her pretty teeth had spaces between them, the travelling lady sniffed and returned to her food.

Only Sam Carpenter noticed the girl slipping in and out from the kitchen stairs and quietly arranging pies and puddings on the sideboard. Leaning towards his father, he asked who the blond beauty in the blue dress might be and learned that she was the daughter of the Gideon Landis they were talking about earlier. The Fox had to have a new cook, the Squire explained, to replace Patience Slack, who threw her belongings into a carpetbag Saturday morning and had last been seen lurching down the road towards Enterprise.

"Your mama wanted a steady one this time," the Squire added. "And at least Landis's daughter ain't likely to dip into the rum."

The moment dessert was finished, the Squire stood up. Leaving his wife and Martha to clear the table with the help of the new girl, he gruffly summoned Sam and Eleanor to follow him to the small, cluttered room he used as his office. It was hardly more than a cubicle, almost filled with an open secretary, the desk spilling over with papers in the Squire's precise hand. Sitting down and resting an elbow among the papers, he pointed Eleanor into the other chair, while Sam stood and fingered his sideburns.

Without wasting time, Will Carpenter said, "Well, Princess,

you've been home three days now, and I'm still waiting to hear what this nonsense is about leaving your husband."

Eleanor's eyes were on her lap as she said stubbornly, "I've left him, and that's that. I thought Aunt Sophie told you."

"Your Aunt Sophie might as well be the sphinx, from all she said in her letter," the Squire shot back. "When she dropped you here, she hardly stayed long enough to use the outhouse, much less explain anything, before she took off again. Prying something out of her is like asking the cat how many canaries it ate before breakfast."

In a steady voice, Eleanor replied, "I hope she told you I'm not going back." Meeting her father's eyes, she announced, "I'm tired of being married to him."

The Squire chuckled sarcastically, and Eleanor flushed, while her brother watched to see if she'd fly into a tantrum. Instead, she held her tongue.

Leaning towards her, the Squire said, "Look here, my girl, you're a woman now, and I'll talk to you straight. I gave you away proper (and it cost me a pretty penny, I'll tell you). Now, what in blazes do you think you're doing? You belong to Alec Johns the same way Gumbo Jim belongs to me, only Gumbo can work his freedom out in another four, five years. But you, Princess," he said, firing his words like explosions, "you're married for good."

As if each word were a pistol shot, Eleanor crumpled. "You don't know what it's like," she said hysterically. "I won't go back!"

Softened as always by his pretty daughter (and possibly, like Sam, remembering her childhood tantrums), the Squire shifted tactics. "Come on now, Nelly," he said in a wheedling voice. "I know young women don't always know what they're taking on with a husband, but they get used to it, and you will too. You just bear with Alec, and after a time you won't mind so much. The shame is just losing that baby, or you'd be settled into a wife easy enough by now."

"But that's not it at all!" Eleanor exclaimed, eyes widening as she caught her father's drift. She glanced at her brother, then tossed her head. "If I have to tell you, it wasn't like that at all—or, anyway, it wasn't for very long." Embarrassed, she fingered her locket and lowered her voice. "Since the first couple months, Alec hasn't had anything to do with me," she said, her face beet red. "One morning, he packed up his brushes and moved down the hall. Since then he's hardly even talked to me—except when we have company." She looked at her father defiantly. "For two years I haven't had anyone to talk to but the hired girl," she said bitterly. "Now do you see why I can't stay married?"

The Squire was shaken by information so different from what he'd expected. Indignant now at the injustice to his little girl, he said slowly, "You mean to tell me Alec Johns hasn't acted the husband to you for two years?" Caught between anger and humiliation, Eleanor nodded.

Never one to miss a nuance, Sam asked quietly, "And who does Alec talk to?"

"That's no problem," Eleanor retorted, her voice brittle with anger. "Remember Gilbert, his old boarding-school friend—the one that used to write those nauseating verses? He lives with us now. He has a bedroom next to Alec's. I hear the two of them laughing and chattering half the night."

"By the Lord Harry, that does it!" exclaimed the Squire, slamming down his fist and sending quills and papers flying. "There's no way I'm sending my little girl back to a man like that! Tell your mother you're to have your old room back, and tell her she'll have to think on making room for your piano."

Jumping from her chair, Eleanor gave her father a hug and hurried to the door, the Squire's scattered papers rustling at her feet. Suddenly she stopped. "Does that mean I can marry someone else now?" she asked.

"We'll see, Princess, we'll see," answered the Squire. A last glance at her brother, and Eleanor left the office, as the Squire sat shaking his head. "There ain't much chance of that," he said as soon as she was gone, "unless I go over and throttle Johns with my bare hands — as I'm sorely tempted. What did that son of Belial have in mind marrying her in the first place, if he didn't mean to act the husband?"

"I could challenge him to a duel," Sam said lightly.

The Squire shook his head. "That's enough nonsense," he rumbled. "We got to think on how to untie your sister — inside the law. Lucky we got a lawyer in the family," he added, with a shrewd look at his son. "Now's the time we'll find out what your fancy education learned you." He motioned towards Eleanor's chair. "I guess I paid enough already for a consultation fee," he said. "Now let's hear what the law has to say."

Prepared by his aunt's letter as well as by certain rumors, in short order Sam laid out Eleanor's situation in the eyes of the law. There was no chance of an annulment, he explained, because of Eleanor's stillborn baby, buried with the rest of the Johns family in a Christiana churchyard. But since, under the circumstances, Alec wasn't likely to want Eleanor back, Sam's advice was that Eleanor stay at the Fox as Mrs. Johns, a lady visiting with her family.

"That's the confoundest fool advice I ever heard," the Squire retorted. Again he slammed his fist, jarring the books above the desk. "You're telling me that Johns has to keep on owning your sister — after what she told us. I tell you, before I let that happen, I'll bribe his hired girl to put arsenic in his toddy. I want you to get your sister unmarried, and that's that."

Sam nodded. "In that case," he said, "we'll have to get a decree of divorce put through the State Assembly. It could be messy unless we get help," he added, raising his eyebrows, "that is, from someone with influence enough to slip it through on the quiet."

The Squire chuckled mirthlessly. "It's good to hear I may get a return yet on my best Madeira. By the way," he added, "where's your bigwig friend McMaster going to spend his Christmas?"

4.

er move to the Fox threw Catherine Landis into a strange
new life. Like everyone in the neighborhood, she knew
the Carpenters and often delivered the butter her mother sold
them when the cows were fresh. Besides, a family so prominent
was a never-ending source of gossip, spread through the countryside by John Skiles on his stops. As a result, the farm families
were proud when Sam went off to Dickinson College and even
more when Eleanor married Alec Johns. Everybody knew that
Miss Carpenter played the piano and sang, painted flowers on
china, and did fancy embroidery, leaving farm women shaking
their heads at such a wealth of time. It wasn't surprising that
Catherine was thoroughly intimidated by Mrs. Carpenter's
grandness and Martha's distance when they took turns super-
vising her cooking.

Except for waiting on table at upstairs meals and climbing at
night to the attic room recently vacated by Patience Slack,
Catherine spent most of her day in the kitchen or the second
floor of the three-story spring house, where much of the food

was prepared. She ate her own meals at a table set for the help in the kitchen. The hired man who farmed for the Squire ate with his family in one of the tenant houses across the road, as Mrs. Belcher did, too. When her asthma wasn't too bad, Mrs. Belcher served customers in the taproom, while her daughters cleaned upstairs rooms. But when she wheezed too badly and couldn't catch her breath or when business was especially brisk, Catherine served in the taproom and drew cider and beer for the customers (stronger drink being dispensed by the Squire or the German redemptioner at the tapster's grate).

When he wasn't hanging around the stables, she had an assistant, Davy McGuire, an undergrown pauper boy of eleven or twelve (he wasn't sure which), whom the Squire got at an auction, promising to give him food and clothing for his service. Davy hauled in wood, emptied spittoons, and mopped the floor with the leavings of the dishwater. Elizabeth had sewed bread-crumbs into Catherine's petticoat to cure homesickness, but Davy helped more because he reminded her of her brothers.

Comfortable as she was with Davy, Catherine wasn't at ease with Gumbo Jim, the young Negro who tended the stables and looked after everything else that needed to be done. Most customers at the Fox were neighbors who knew her father more or less, but Jim reminded her of the bogeyman who frightened bad children. A few people of color lived in the country, mostly as servants in wealthy families, but they were beyond Catherine's experience. Now, eating beside a man with a shiny brown skin, she tried not to be nervous. Davy worshipped Jim and hung at his heels like a skinny white shadow, but the stable man was quiet around Catherine, only answering direct questions—and then Catherine couldn't understand what he said. She was shocked, a week or two after she moved to the Fox, to hear him talking German with a redheaded customer.

When she asked him about it at supper, Jim smiled and cocked an eyebrow. "I been here since I was ten years old," he said, "and I ain't too dumb to pick up somethin' here and there." After that Catherine started to relax with him and learned that he had been born in Virginia and sent north with his mother as part of an inheritance. His mother died before working out her freedom, and Jim now had four years and five months (and thirteen days, he added) till he finished his service at twenty-eight. Curious, Catherine asked what he was going to do when he was free.

"Maybe go to the city," he said. "Get me work cleanin' chimneys. Ike Gilmore, he got a business and always ready to take on a good man. Cleanin' chimneys is good work for niggers," he added slyly, "cause the soot don't show." Davy almost fell off his chair laughing, but Catherine was more confused than ever by Gumbo Jim.

If life at the Fox was leisurely for some, the downstairs was always in a bustle. Davy was supposed to fetch in provisions, but he was usually in the stables, and Catherine carried most of them in from the outbuildings where they were stored (though the Squire himself always brought in the meat from where it hung under lock and key in the top of the spring house). Tuesdays and Fridays she baked mountains of bread and pies in the oven next to the spring house, and at night chores didn't end till dried vegetables were put to soak and arrangements taken care of for the next day. By the end of her day Catherine looked forward to climbing the stairs to bed, often to the sound of piano music floating up from the parlor where Eleanor Johns was playing by candlelight.

It was early December, and after a day hectic from putting up meat from late butchering on top of everything else, Catherine hurried to get into her nightgown. The chimney by the wall didn't help against the sharp cold, and she couldn't wait to make a nest under the comforter and go to sleep. Suddenly a rap on the door raised chilly prospects of lectures from Mrs. Carpenter for using a smidgeon too much butter or not leaning down the breakfast scrapple with enough cornmeal. Shivering with cold, Catherine put on her nightbonnet and opened the door, to see, of all people, Eleanor Johns. Mrs. Johns seldom left the upstairs parlor, and till now Catherine had caught only glimpses of her.

"You weren't sleeping, were you?" Eleanor asked, and walked in without waiting for an answer. Catherine shook her head. "I know you're Catherine," Eleanor said brightly and sat down on the bed, while Catherine slowly tied the strings of her nightbonnet, waiting to hear the purpose of her visit.

"You do have a small room, don't you?" Eleanor remarked, glancing at the sloping walls as though Catherine had chosen them for herself. Before she could answer, Eleanor chirped, "I thought we could talk. There aren't many people to talk to here—at least the kind you can tell things to—people our age, I mean."

While Catherine stared, her guest bubbled on, making up for her own silence. "I know I'm older than you," Eleanor continued in quick, staccato phrases, "but only two or three years. Did you know I'm twenty-one? I can't talk to Martha," she added, fidgeting with her locket. "She's always been jealous—and I'm all alone here." As though she'd been wound up and the spring had run down, she stopped. Eleanor studied Catherine's face, and Catherine said hesitantly, "Maybe we could some other time, only it's awful late now."

Relieved at a response, Eleanor beamed at her. "Not really," she said brightly. "It's not even ten-thirty. We have lots of time."

"But Mrs. Johns," Catherine said, "you sleep till eight in the morning. I have to be up before five. If ten-thirty is early for you, it's the middle of the night for me."

Eleanor's eyes opened in surprise. "Is it really?" she asked. She flashed an impish smile. "I'll tell you what," she said. "I'll let you go to bed if you call me Eleanor. Nelly would be even better," she added. "That's what Papa calls me."

Too tired to argue and afraid of being rude, Catherine looked longingly at her bed. The floor was cold against her feet, and she was shivering. "Eleanor," she said numbly.

Eleanor look relieved. "We will be friends. I know it." She stood up and hugged her shoulders. "My, but it's cold up here," she remarked, as though she'd just noticed. In another minute she swept out the door, leaving Catherine to puzzle over the strange visit in the very few minutes before she fell asleep.

December at the Fox was especially hectic. The early part of the month saw an election in the upstairs parlor, where Eleanor's piano was pushed into a corner for the occasion, while Catherine, forced to serve in the taproom by Mrs. Belcher's asthma, wondered over the posters extolling some candidates and reviling others. She was even busier a few weeks later, serving toasts to Andrew Jackson and the triumph of democracy.

Her father made a point of stopping in once or twice a week, to look over the newspaper, he said, though half the time he picked up the wrong one, and Catherine knew he couldn't read English. Sometimes he talked with the Squire, lines wrinkling his forehead. In his brief exchanges with Catherine, he told her that Peter had taken well to wagonmaking. Her mother wasn't well, Gideon said, but could do without her through the winter. When Catherine asked how the new house was coming along, his forehead wrinkled again. "It's getting there," was as much as he said.

After her night visit, Eleanor Johns began dropping into the kitchen or the spring house where Catherine was working. At first she was a nuisance, till Catherine started giving her the light chores Davy should have done, if only to keep her from being underfoot. The first time she handed a basin of carrots to Eleanor, asking if she'd mind scraping them, she expected Mrs. Johns to sweep from the room. Instead, Eleanor seemed to think helping in the kitchen was a kind of lark. Obediently, she followed Catherine's directions, chattering the while about guests and visitors, current fashions, and the upcoming holiday, when her brother was coming to stay and bringing an old college friend. After half an hour or so, Catherine would notice the quiet and turn to see that Eleanor had slipped away, leaving the work half done.

To her surprise, Catherine found herself looking forward to

Eleanor's visits. Martha and Mrs. Carpenter hardly talked to her, except in the one case to give instructions and in the other to admonish her to be more frugal. Eleanor was at least company, with the flutter of her talk. And Eleanor did all the talking, though occasionally she might say, "Catherine, I want to know all about you. Do you have a beau?" But the minute Catherine started to answer, Eleanor interrupted, perhaps to chatter about a novel she was reading, perhaps to describe the dress she was planning on wearing to a Christmas party.

In all, Eleanor Johns was airy as a butterfly—most of the time. The exceptions were fits of silence, when Catherine would turn to see her staring into the fire. If she spoke to her then, Eleanor would smile vaguely and, perhaps for the tenth time, ask how many little brothers Catherine had. "I almost had a little boy," she said once, fingering her locket. Other times she broke her silence to praise Catherine effusively and thank her for her friendship.

"Promise you'll always be my friend," Eleanor said after one of her pensive fits. By then, Catherine thought of Eleanor with the indulgence she felt about Davy and her little brothers. Besides, she knew that when she left the Fox, her path wasn't likely to cross that of the brilliant Mrs. Johns. Of course they'd stay friends, she answered soothingly.

"No," Eleanor said. "I mean a real friend—one I can count on to help me if I need it."

Nervous from the hysterical edge in Eleanor's voice, Catherine answered evasively. "People are all supposed to help each other," she said.

"That's no answer!" Eleanor flashed out. Bursting into tears, she rushed from the room.

She didn't reappear for nearly a week, and Catherine missed Eleanor's chatter. If, as she claimed, Eleanor had no one else to talk to, hardly anyone at the Fox talked to her, either. When Eleanor showed up in the spring house while Catherine was kneading bread, Catherine greeted her warmly.

"I don't know why you're glad to see me," Eleanor said

airily. "It's not as though we're friends."

Catherine was taken aback. "I never said we weren't," she replied, stung by Eleanor's manner. The only sound for the next few minutes was the thump of dough.

"Well?" Eleanor finally said. Hurt and puzzled, Catherine looked at her inquiringly. "Are you going to be my friend or aren't you?" Eleanor demanded.

"I guess so," Catherine answered, feeling homesick and deserted.

"Say it then," Eleanor insisted.

"I'll be your friend, Eleanor," Catherine pronounced, half suspecting that she'd been tricked.

Her face glowing, Eleanor gave Catherine an effusive hug. "I knew I could trust you!" she exclaimed, inadvertently spilling flour over both of them. Catherine cleaned up after her guest and set her to rolling out scraps of dough, and soon Eleanor was chattering as usual, yet again asking Catherine about her little brothers and yet again interrupting before Catherine could answer.

Besides Eleanor Johns, the other people Catherine had to talk with were Davy and, occasionally, Mrs. Belcher, whose conversation was mostly wheezes and complaints. Whenever the taproom was busy, Mrs. Belcher would waddle into the kitchen and drop into a chair. "I'll be all right if I can just sigh," she'd gasp between wheezes. After a minute or so of panting like a bellows, she'd let out a long groan. "That's better now," she'd say before heaving herself up and waddling back to the taproom.

When Mrs. Belcher couldn't sigh and Catherine had to take care of the taproom, the respectable farmers mostly ignored her. As for outsiders, the Squire, who presided there most evenings, was careful enough about the Fox's reputation that he put a quick stop to any impudence to his waiting girl.

The most regular customer was John Skiles, who could be found any time of morning, afternoon, or evening sitting on the settee next to the fire and replenishing his supply of gossip or, if he was lucky, his mug, in return for news he'd picked up at one end of the township or the other. He talked to Catherine more than the other customers did, invariably trapping her with questions about her family and asking when her father was going to pay Owen Rees. "I know that one, and he don't like waiting on his money," Skiles might add. To avoid him and his questions, Catherine tried to be very busy or, at worst, not to understand him, as though she didn't know enough English to follow what he said.

But in spite of customers like Skiles, it was exciting to be beside the Old Road after the isolation of the farm. Muddy, rutted, and difficult as it was in comparison with the Pike a few miles away, it carried its quota of traffic. Local stages still used it, and it was the favorite route for drovers urging on herds of cows or pigs from the West to market in Philadelphia or Wilmington. Such dirty, bedraggled travellers, of course, were not welcome at an inn like the Fox, hierarchies of rank and importance strictly governing where travellers could get food and lodging.

In that the Fox might have seemed anomalous, from the Conestoga wagons now and then standing in the courtyard. But Will Carpenter didn't set his clock ahead for nothing. Thirty-five years before, genteel business had fallen off badly. Because of the new Pike (acclaimed across the Union as an engineering marvel), the Fox had been in a bad way when his father died, and Will had had to scramble ruthlessly against debts and assorted mortgages.

Part of the new Squire's strategy was to take advantage of what traffic remained on the Old Road but to keep the upstairs for gentlemen and ladies. Of course, Will Carpenter didn't stoop to turning the Fox into a wagon stand for regulars, as professional drivers were known. Opening the inn to men who worked for, say, the Line Wagon Company, would have put a stop to custom from gentlemen and seriously affected business in the taproom.

Still, mindful of local farmers who kept the upstairs of the

Fox afloat through regular visits below, the Squire passed on word that he wouldn't object to stops from their sons, nephews, and cousins, the militia wagoners. They were farmers earning cash through the winter or their sons seeing the world before they settled on farms of their own. The Old Road was a favorite of theirs, in spite of mires, ruts, and occasional tree stumps, the extra time and work made up for by cheap tolls.

As a result, through fall and winter occasional wagoners stopped by day for a sup of beer to wash down their bread and cheese and at night to sleep beside their wagons or, when it was especially cold, in front of the taproom fire. Most of the wagoners were single and from families like Catherine's, and they studied her shyly as she served them. Only one, a lanky young man with a shock of red hair, was flippant to her. Worse, when he wanted beer, he shouted for the pretty blond, inspiring Mrs. Belcher to lose her breath in wheezy laughter and raising Catherine's temper enough that she stamped her foot and refused to go into the taproom. From the loud laughter whenever he stopped at the Fox, Catherine set him down as a rowdy and stayed in the kitchen when she heard his voice, though Mrs. Belcher gave her a crafty look and wheezed, "I got a notion somebody's sweet on somebody," winking so hard that her eye disappeared in folds of fat. Catherine disliked the redheaded wagoner all the more — until she found a reason to change her mind.

In late December the weather changed, and the Old Road turned into a swamp, trapping carriages and coating travellers with mud. It was the Saturday before Christmas, and Catherine was looking forward to visiting home. Through the day the sun shone fiercely, making her sweat over her work, though the early sunset brought an instant chill. A wagon had stopped before dark, when it would be too dangerous to travel. From the pump Catherine could see the driver grooming his horses and setting planks under the wagon wheels to keep from being frozen in by morning. With distaste she noticed that it was the rowdy Dutchman, his hair flaming redder than ever against his blue wagon.

She hurried back to the kitchen to find Eleanor Johns perched on a stool by the fire. Eleanor was especially talkative and bubbled on cheerfully about plans for the holidays and her brother's visit, but her clear, light voice stopped in mid-sentence, succeeded by a scream.

Startled, Catherine turned from the kettle she was setting to heat, slopping water in her hurry.

It took Catherine a moment to see what Eleanor was staring at, a snake lying in the corner of the fireplace. Copperheads weren't plentiful, but every country child learned to avoid places where they might shelter. Roused by the warm day, this one had found a crack in the chimney and followed it to find more heat. As it basked by the fire Catherine had startled it, and its beady eyes were fixed on her from a head raised above a bronze coil.

Eleanor's scream continued in thin, intermittent shrieks, while Catherine stood motionless. She barely noticed Mrs. Belcher, who waddled into the room, then out again, wheezing for help in asthmatic gasps. Next came a rush of footsteps and excited voices. Then a voice cut through the others, telling her in German to jump away at the signal. *"Versteh?"* the voice asked, and repeated the instructions. *"Ya,"* Catherine breathed. Seconds later a whip cracked across the room, and the snake flew against the wall of the fireplace, as the voice shouted, *"Aber schnell!"*

Catherine leaped away. Then, with weak legs, she leaned against the kitchen table and watched a gaggle of men from the taproom converge on the fireplace. One snatched up a poker. Another flourished the loggerhead used for heating flip. The men jiggled about, trying to land blows on the cornered snake.

Eleanor's shrieks still echoed through the room, as more footsteps thundered down the stairs. Sam Carpenter burst through the door, followed by the Squire, his greetings to son and guest cut short by Eleanor's scream. Sam seized his sister's shoulders and shook her. "Stop it, Eleanor, stop it!" he shouted.

He dragged her across the room, thrust her against his father, and hurriedly joined the scramble at the fireplace.

The redheaded wagoner stood by the taproom door, the long whip he used for guiding his horses poised to use again if he saw the chance. Catherine had seen wagoners playing their whips over their teams, but till now she hadn't appreciated their skill. Meanwhile, the confusion at the fireplace hid the snake, and all she could see was John Skiles bouncing behind one or the other of the hunters and calling directions, invariably too late.

"Hey! Watch out for that there crack!" Skiles shouted, just as the hubbub ceased.

"Drat it," said the tall thin man waving the loggerhead. "Why'd you let him get past, Andy? You rutched back, just when you should of smashed him a good one."

"What happened?" the redheaded wagoner asked, striding to the fireplace.

"It wonders me, Jake," responded the man with the poker, "unless that fireplace is hexed. That skinny little crack don't look big enough for a grass snake even. First off, you couldn't see the head, then swish — and the whole thing got all."

The redhead was studying the crack, while the others moved back to give Sam Carpenter a view.

"You'd better have that crack sealed up," Sam said to the Squire, who was still calming his daughter.

"You got any lime around, and I'll see to it," spoke up the wagoner. "I've done plastering, and I'll do it right, if I have to barber my team to get hair for it."

"Jake'll do it, too," spoke up Skiles, nodding approvingly. "He got a special receipt he learned from his pap."

Catherine shivered and sat down at the table.

"You all right?" the wagoner asked, concern in his voice. Catherine nodded and swallowed to keep back tears. She looked up and gave a start. Behind Jake Good and in the shadow of the stairs a man stood surveying the room, fixing his eyes on one figure after another, first her, then the men at the fireplace, and stopping on Eleanor.

"Oh, there you are, Nick!" exclaimed Sam Carpenter. "You missed the excitement my father just staged to announce your visit!"

5.

Nicholas McMaster was pleased when Mrs. Carpenter's flowery note arrived, inviting him to spend Christmas at the Fox. His parents had been dead for some years, and though he had two sisters and a brother in western Pennsylvania, Christmas was no longer a family ritual. Since he'd moved to Lancaster and set up his law practice near the square, he'd kept a simple bachelor establishment, practical and economical, especially now that he spent much of his year in Harrisburg while the State Assembly was in session. A week in the country would be a pleasant break, as well as an opportunity to test political currents in the county.

As an especially eligible bachelor, McMaster moved freely in the better circles around Lancaster and hadn't been in danger of spending Christmas alone. An invitation from the Carpenters, however, had a special attraction in the company of Sam who, though two years his junior at college, had been as close an intimate as he allowed himself there. As an added enticement, Sam mentioned that his sister Eleanor was spending a month or so with the family. A pretty woman was always an attraction, especially (enemies noted) when the woman happened to be safely married, allowing for gallantries without any risk of deeper involvement.

As a lawyer and politician, however, McMaster knew that every favor involves corresponding obligations. This one, he calculated, he'd partly discharged in advance by his carefully dropped information to Sam about the route of the new railroad. Still, a visit of eight days might involve more, which he didn't necessarily object to. Power was based on ties, and closer association with the Carpenters would strengthen his political base in Lampeter.

His visit to the kitchen just after he arrived made it clear that Eleanor Johns was sure to add spice to his visit. With her dark hair and white skin, she was remarkably pretty, and to his mind women were most attractive when they showed their vulnerability. The plain sister, Martha, was a sullen brute but seemed to know her place and wasn't likely to be a nuisance. And what a lovely country girl the Squire had working in the kitchen, as blooming and golden as Eleanor was delicate and brunette. According to Sam, she came from a respectable family a mile or so away and disappeared every other Sunday to attend Mennonite services. McMaster never forgot that if power lay in the hands of people like Will Carpenter, votes came from the less exalted, and he counted on getting to know the pretty cook, just as he planned to make regular visits to the taproom as an investment against future elections.

McMaster passed his first evening at the Fox without female company, the fascinating Eleanor having been half carried to her room by her father, who ordered his wife and elder daughter not to leave Nelly till she got over her hysteria. When the Squire returned to the parlor, the three men settled down to a comfortable evening's conversation, helped on by a selection of fine Madeira.

They'd chatted for some time, McMaster taking the opportunity to ferret out local concerns, before they moved on to national ones. "I don't much know about this Jackson," the Squire was saying, shaking his head. "Adams maybe was a Yankee, but with him in Washington, at least you knew it wasn't a bunch of rabble running things. What with all these Irish over here digging canals and begging for table leavings, him in office is just one more sign how the Union's going to the dogs. I doubt it will hold together another four years."

McMaster smiled. "You may be surprised when the General gets the reins in his hands," he said, arching his fingers. "He knows how to get votes, but he may not turn out to be quite the leveller you think. The poet says, 'Be not the first to lay the old aside,' and Jackson isn't likely to, whatever he lets people think."

Just then someone tapped on the door, and Mrs. Carpenter stuck her head into the room. "Oh, please, Mr. McMaster, make yourself at home," she said, delighted as he rose and bowed stiffly. "I wouldn't interrupt for the world, Mr. Carpenter, but I thought you'd like to know that your daughter has finally gone to sleep. A dose of laudanum finally calmed her, but just to make you happy I told Martha to sit with her. She'll be herself in the morning—or as much as she's likely to be," she added, "with this business hanging over her head."

The Squire nodded. "That will do, Mother," he growled. "You can take yourself off now and let us get on with our business"—business being what men did when women weren't with them.

"I hope your room is comfortable," Mrs. Carpenter added to McMaster before curtsying and disappearing again.

Masculine hegemony restored, the three men sipped their Madeira, while McMaster waited to hear whether or not his host would follow up on his wife's interesting remark. It was Sam who did.

"You might as well know, Nick," he said, "my sister's situation as Mrs. Johns is—how should I put it?—not exactly viable any longer."

"You can say more than that, and it will be a sight short of the truth," muttered the Squire. At a gesture from his son, however, he let the family legal expert explain Eleanor's situation in suitably abstract language, nodding appreciatively the while at the long words that rolled off Sam's tongue.

"So you see, Nick," Sam concluded, "our problem is how we can dissolve Eleanor's marriage without any more fuss than we have to."

Head cocked to one side, McMaster had been listening carefully, interrupting Sam's narrative now and then with terse questions. Satisfied that he had the facts of the case, he took a sip of Madeira, pleased that the payment for his country holiday—and especially access to the Squire's wine cellar—was within reason, though it was high enough that in return the Carpenters, including Eleanor, would be in his debt.

"There are difficulties," he said slowly, swirling his wine in time to the ticking of the Squire's clock. "As you know, every divorce petition has to be documented with substantive reasons before the Assembly will consider it. And even then," he added, "passage isn't automatic, especially if it's contested."

"Sam says they pass ten or twelve a year," the Squire interrupted gruffly, "and women can even bring 'em."

"That's true," McMaster answered. "The Commonwealth, after all, isn't England. Still, the business has to be done in full assembly and goes into the public record, and there may be a certain amount of—what should I say?—curiosity. Even a lady like Miss Eleanor could find herself uncomfortable."

Will Carpenter was shaken. "My girl's suffered enough already," he said. "On top of everything else, I won't have her called a scarlet woman."

Unperturbed, Sam poured more Madeira into McMaster's glass. "We heard wonders about how you managed the governor's last campaign," he remarked.

It was six of one to half a dozen of the other whether McMaster's smile came from the wine or the compliment. "I'll think about what I can manage for Miss Eleanor," he said before downing the wine and excusing himself to deal with some correspondence.

The next day, to McMaster's disappointment, Eleanor stayed in her room, her meals delivered by her plain sister. Martha Carpenter looked more and more sour to McMaster's discriminating eyes, especially when the rest of the family put on their finery and set off to church in Lancaster, where McMaster sat with his hosts in the Carpenters' box pew. It wasn't until late in the evening that he finally managed to encounter Eleanor Johns.

Following his habit, he was in his room with a sheaf of documents he intended to master before the Assembly reconvened. He'd gotten halfway through a brief on property rights when he heard the faint tinkling of a piano, almost immediately broken off at the booming of the Squire's clock. After eleven strokes, the music resumed.

Laying aside his papers, McMaster picked up his candle and went into the hall. From here he could make out the faint thread of a woman's voice, which, when he reached the staircase, resolved itself into a familiar tune. Smiling to himself, he made his way down the stairs. First putting out his candle, he quietly opened the parlor door.

The fire had gone out, and a branched candlestick on the piano gave the only light in the chilly room, illuminating the slender figure of Eleanor Johns. Absorbed in Dr. Arne's music, she was singing in a thin, sweet voice as, from the dark, McMaster fixed his eyes on her. A white shawl across her shoulders, Eleanor looked as ethereal as the Ariel she was singing about.

While McMaster stood swaying his head in time with the music, Eleanor stiffened. Her voice faltered, and the keys clashed discordantly. Wide-eyed, she whirled to face the door.

"Please forgive me," McMaster said, stepping forward. "My candle went out, and I thought there might be a fire in here."

Eleanor put a hand to her breast and laughed nervously. "You gave me a fright," she said. Recovering herself, she patted her hair and adjusted her skirts.

Remembering that beautiful women have to be flattered for their brains and talent, McMaster said, "To make a confession, I didn't really come because of the candle. I heard the music and couldn't stay away. You have a wonderful voice, Miss Eleanor, the best I've heard outside a concert hall."

But Eleanor was used to being petted and praised, thanks to her father. Instead of appreciating the compliment, she arched an eyebrow and remarked, "Everyone else says so, too." She looked at McMaster coyly and burst into a laugh.

McMaster smiled. "I hope you'll sing more, now that I've found you."

"Of course, if you want me to," Eleanor answered, carelessly fingering the keys. "Do you have any favorites?"

"I can think of one or two," McMaster said. "Do you know Polly's song, when she tells her family about Macheath? I've always liked that one."

Eleanor smiled archly. "Of course I do," she said, preening. "You mean, 'Can Love be Control'd by Advice.' I've had that music forever, ever since—" She broke off and added quietly, "It was a present someone gave me once." She played the opening measures, rushing the tempo, then stopped abruptly. "I have a better idea," she said with a brittle smile. "What about some duets? Polly and Macheath have some nice ones."

Studying her through half-closed eyes, McMaster turned down his mouth in mock despair. "I wish I could," he answered, "but to tell the truth, much as I appreciate the talent, I don't have it. I have to confess that I'm tone deaf."

"In that case," said Eleanor, whirling on her stool, "I won't play for you."

"—And will have to entertain me with conversation instead," McMaster immediately countered, "as the least of your obligations to a guest."

Eleanor watched him closely but didn't object as he drew a chair close to the piano.

"Am I right in guessing that Gay's music was a present from your husband?"

Eleanor flushed. "He wasn't my husband then, really, and he's not now," she said emphatically.

"But there must have been a time," McMaster replied. Eleanor turned her face away, and he continued, "I only want to let you know that I'll look after this business for you. It's lucky that I'm in a position that I can." Eleanor remained silent. After a pause he said, "I'll handle your case with as much delicacy as I can—under the circumstances."

Eleanor's face was still turned away. "What circumstances do you mean?" she asked softly.

McMaster sighed. "My dear Miss Eleanor," he answered. "We can't forget the democracy in this great republic. The people like to know what their legislators do."

Eleanor turned to him with frightened eyes. "Tell me what you mean," she said. "You're telling me there's going to be a scandal! That's it, isn't it?" McMaster didn't answer.

Eleanor hid her face in her hands. "I can't stand much more," she said, so quietly that McMaster could barely hear her.

"My dear, my dear," he said, putting a hand on her shoulder. "Don't fret yourself. Haven't I said I'll look after everything?"

Too upset to hear him, Eleanor rocked back and forth in her misery, while McMaster spoke firmly but gently in her ear. "I have some influence," he said, "and I can drop a word to the right people. It's not easy, and it's not done often. But still, it's possible." Eleanor was listening intently, as he knew from her stillness. Withdrawing his hand, he continued, "Some transactions have been known to disappear from public records."

"Disappear?" Eleanor whispered.

"Oh, the legislation is still official enough," McMaster assured her, "—even if only a few members happened to be sitting when it passed. The question is simply whether or not the secretary wrote it into the minutes. And he has occasionally been—how shall I say it?—absent-minded."

"I see," Eleanor breathed, looking up, her face suddenly hopeful.

45

"In that case, of course, no one can monger gossip, where no one even knows what's happened." He leaned back in his chair and smiled. "So you see, your reputation is safe as long as I look after things for you."

Eleanor rubbed a tear from her cheek and smiled radiantly. "Mr. McMaster, if you do this for me, I won't know how to thank you."

"You can start by calling me Nick," he said.

Before she could answer, the clock struck the half hour. "I have to go," Eleanor said, rising hastily. Before he could stop her, she flitted from the room, leaving behind a faint smell of roses.

Thoughtfully, McMaster lit his candle from the candelabrum, snuffed the candles in it one by one, and made his way upstairs, satisfied with the evening's conversation.

6.

*A*fter Catherine's visit home, she didn't want to go back to the Fox, especially Christmas week, when, instead, she should have been home getting surprises ready for her little brothers and helping her mother with holiday baking. Besides, a month at the Fox had rubbed off its glamour, and she was thoroughly homesick.

Her discontent was partly sparked by a sense that things weren't well with her family. Owen Rees had packed up his trowel and level, leaving behind the shell of the new house, but the inside was only a skeleton of beams, since Gideon instantly stopped work on it to spend his time hauling stone from his quarry. He'd been lucky enough to sell some to the city, where breaking it to dress city streets occupied its thieves and debtors and kept them warm in the cold that settled in again Christmas week.

Catherine was warm enough, at least during the day, one advantage to working at the kitchen fireplace. But the cold weather made it hard for Mrs. Belcher to sigh, and she sent word that she was laid up with the asthma (as she usually was on holidays, Mrs. Carpenter remarked testily). The upshot was that Catherine found herself spending as much time in the taproom as the kitchen, especially for the first half of the week, when the whole countryside seemed bent on squeezing into the Fox in the three days before Christmas. Davy was constantly scuttling in with armloads of firewood, and Gumbo Jim hustled to look after the horses, which steamed in the air as he walked them in the courtyard. He brought their sharp smell with him in the snatched minutes when he could duck into the kitchen to warm himself at the fire, which he huddled over, shivering with blue lips.

Homesick as she was, Catherine felt sorry for Jim and heated cider for him, though he remained taciturn and distant. One evening when she was especially harried from being called into the taproom while she was getting supper ready for upstairs, he got in her way, and she snapped at him — and instantly regretted it.

"I'm mighty sorry, Missy," Gumbo said. "My head ain't thinkin' right, and my feet ain't movin' right, 'cause I got a worry." Ready to bite out her tongue, Catherine apologized profusely and asked what ailed him.

"You see, Missy, I got me a brother still in Virginia, and the master wants to sell him, 'cause Cassius, he's one lippy nigger. And Cassius, he says, before he's going to the rice fields, he'll chop off his hand." To clarify, Gumbo clenched his right hand over an imaginary blade and slammed it across his left arm. "Just like that," Gumbo said. "He'll do it, too," he added.

Catherine watched in horror, but after a minute her face relaxed. "You're only funning me, Jim," she said. "You can't know that."

Jim looked at her sadly. "There's ways," he said. "I know what I know, but I ain't sayin' how." Refusing to say more, he downed his cider and returned to the stable, leaving Catherine shaken by the glimpse he'd given her of his side of the world.

In the days before Christmas she barely saw Eleanor Johns

but was too busy to miss her, all of her energy taken up with dashing back and forth between kitchen and taproom, kitchen and pump, and kitchen and upstairs, not to mention spring house and bake oven. Eleanor's time now, she gathered, was taken up with her brother and his guest, whom Mrs. Johns accompanied on rides over frozen roads to visit friends and view the countryside.

Eleanor flitted into the kitchen now and again, usually with some request, but she didn't stay to chatter in her usual, inconsequential way. The little she did say was invariably about Nicholas McMaster—his attentions, his trips abroad, and his invitations to parties in Lancaster he planned to attend after he left the Fox on Sunday.

Sometimes Catherine saw him, too. McMaster made regular forays into the taproom, usually through the kitchen. If there was enough bustle that she didn't hear his soft footsteps (as there was during most of Christmas week), she might suddenly feel uncomfortable and wheel sharply to see his eyes fixed on her from the door. He disconcerted her, and when he spoke, she answered awkwardly and made excuses to fetch in supplies or answer calls from the taproom, where she felt his half-closed eyes following her as she filled tankards and served customers.

In the taproom he moved from table to table, greeting people or introducing himself with a stiff dignity which set him apart from the country people even more than his expensive clothes. He usually sat down with one knot of people or another, listening more than talking, and drinking even less. Shortly, rounds complete, he disappeared once more into the upper reaches of the Fox, leaving the drinkers smiling over their mugs at how accessible the man was they'd elected to speak for them in the State Assembly.

"Yes siree," said John Skiles, nodding over the drink McMaster had bought him before he left. "They can call him Old Nick if they want to, but that McMaster has my vote." He took a long pull from his mug and sat back against the wood settee, his paunch resting between his legs and his mug waving in time with his words. "You can trust a fella like that. Why, he can shussle anything he wants through the Assembly, but he ain't too stuck up to talk to a man. From what I hear, he owns property enough, he could buy out the Squire yet, and still have plenty left."

"Ach Chon, he ain't that rich," spoke up the man at the other end of the settee, a fellow as tall and thin as Skiles was short and fat. "From what I hear tell, he didn't have two cents to rub together when he come to Lancaster ten, twelve years ago."

"Ten, twelve years ago don't count." Skiles's eyes almost folded into his cheeks from his smile. "I've heard from this one and from that one," he pronounced. "That McMaster, him being a lawyer and all, he knows who's being sold out and how to pick up a bargain. Why, he must own half the city by now — and half the county, too, if you score it up."

"That don't sound to me like a Christian way of doing things," objected a man in a Windsor chair next to the settee and that much farther from the fire. "It ain't Christian or right, takin' advantage of them that's down."

"If you think folks get ahead from doin' the Christian thing, you got another thing comin'," Skiles declared. "Why, these squires around the county weren't nothin' different from you and me fifty years back. They're the ones figured out the smart way soon enough and learned to do a little steppin' on people. And that's how they got to be squires," he finished, flourishing his mug.

"That still don't make it right," insisted the man in the Windsor chair. "Folks go broke farming easy enough, when crops is bad and their money gets all, without they get sold out and don't get nothin' for their place, yet."

The tall man next to Skiles on the settee sputtered over his mug. "I'd maybe worry on folks doin' the Christian thing, too, if I was in your shoes, Cattle Andy, and still loadin' my fields with gypsum, thinkin' to make crops grow. It wonders me you ain't been sold out yet."

"Gypsum still beats lime," Cattle Andy said stubbornly.

"And from what I hear tell, there's one that puts lime on his fields as is closer than me to gettin' sold out."

Tall and short bench sitters leaned forward. Taking his time to explain, Cattle Andy aimed a squirt of tobacco juice at the spittoon, wiped his mouth with the back of his hand, and stretched out his legs.

"What I hear," he said finally, "is that somebody pretty close to here got a big bill due, and the party owed to ain't happy at not gettin' his money when it's promised. In fact, what I hear is that the party what's owed the money to says, if he don't get hisself what's owed him, he's thinkin' of clappin' the party doin' the owin' in jail for debt."

Cattle Andy's pride, however, didn't last long. "Ach, I heard that a week since," said the tall man. "Everyone knows Rees wants his pay, and Landis is strapped on account of the money due him gettin' held up. If you don't got nothin' newer than that to tell of, you better set yourself down and read a newspaper. Beside," he added pointedly, "that Landis is a go-getter — knows better than to put gypsum on his fields. I'll eat my hat if he don't manage to scramble up the money to pay Rees, most likely with that quarry of his."

Sitting like a fat Buddah with his stomach waiting to be rubbed, John Skiles smiled beatifically. "Only problem is," he said, drawing out the words to make sure he had his friends' attention, "might be that quarry ain't his no more."

"Come on, Chon," said the tall man. "How couldn't it be Landis's when it's in the middle of Landis's field? You're all ferhexed and ferhuddled."

"Maybe I am and maybe I ain't," said Skiles. He lifted his empty mug above his head and jiggled it to call for a refill, then waited till he'd taken another pull from it before he went on with his latest gossip.

"Now, you know where Landis's quarry is, smack in the field next to that parcel he sold off to Miles Wilson. He maybe ain't got paid for it yet, but that land sure ain't his no more."

"If you ain't got no better than that to tell, you might as well hush up," Cattle Andy broke in. "Everybody knows that, ain't so Hen?" he asked, appealing to the tall man.

"Now, wait on me," Skiles ordered. "If I didn't know more than that, I wouldn't be sittin' here." His companions looked skeptical, and he went on, "Wilson's will needs executed, and the Squire here's executin' it, ain't?"

"Yeah," the other two agreed unenthusiastically, drawing the word into two syllables.

"Well then," Skiles continued, "what if the Squire put Mr. Sam into checking out old deeds and boundaries, and what if Mr. Sam found out, say, one of them there predicants, and, him bein' a lawyer and all, what if he proved some lines ain't where they was a hundred years back?" Skiles gave a flourish with his mug. "Could even be," he pronounced, "that quarry ain't Landis's no more and he sold it off sort of accidental like, along with the land he sold Wilson."

Tall Hen whistled. "Well I'll be chiggered," he said. "If them lawyers don't beat all. I guess Mr. Sam's smart enough, he could prove a cow's got six legs if he wanted to."

Beaming with satisfaction, Skiles took a swig from his mug, but Cattle Andy leaned forward. "That ain't Christian, and it ain't right!" he exclaimed. "You're sayin' Landis is goin' to get his quarry stole, ain't?"

"It ain't stealin' if it ain't illegal," declared Skiles. "Like I was sayin', you got to be smart to get ahead in this world. Ain't so, Hen?" he asked, appealing to his tall companion.

"Maybe so and maybe not," Tall Hen answered. He looked at their companion on the chair. "Leastways, if I was you, Cattle Andy," he said, "and worried over gettin' et up by those rich folks, I'd stop buying gypsum and start liming my fields, onct."

7.

The cold moderated a bit Wednesday, Christmas Eve, and clots of snow fell all morning. By mid-afternoon the fox smiling from the board above the words "Proprietor, W. Carpenter, Esq." would have disappeared in a snowbank if he had jumped down from the sign and tried to get to the porch of the inn. He probably envied the longer legs of his predecessor, the British General Wolfe, who had been hastily painted over during the Revolution, as soon as it was clear which way the tide was running. If you looked carefully, you could still see the faint outline of a stiff British presence standing behind the fox's left ear, possibly one reason the sly fellow was smiling, ruminating over secrets past and present.

Outside the inn, Gumbo Jim and the men from the tenant houses were digging at a bank of snow, which, in the inscrutable way of snowdrifts had filled the lane and blocked the way to the courtyard. Inside the Fox, Eleanor Johns snapped shut the novel she was reading in the parlor and said, "This has to be the dullest book I've ever read. I don't know when I've been so bored."

Without raising his eyes from the chessboard between him and Nicholas McMaster, Sam Carpenter said languidly, "That's what comes of spending your time on bad romances. You can't appreciate a good book when you do pick one up."

"You're reading Scott, aren't you, Miss Eleanor?" asked McMaster, turning his half-closed eyes on her. "I thought you liked his books."

"That was *Ivanhoe*," Eleanor replied peevishly. "It had knights and romance and lots of adventure, but this is all about some peasant woman. Why, she's not even pretty, and she won't tell an honest fib even to save her own sister's life. I've never read anything so stupid and unbelievable."

"Eleanor's a great fan of Ann Radcliff," Sam remarked, as he studied the chessboard to the steady ticking of the Squire's clock, where a full moon looked down at them from the semicircle above the dial. "There. That may do," he said, as he finally moved his queen.

McMaster's hand flicked out. "Checkmate," he said, moving his knight.

"Now, how did you find that opening?" Sam exclaimed. "You do it every time, and I never figure out how, though I know you lead me along to just where you've got me. I can beat most people, but I have to admit, Nick, you're one too many for me. You have to get it from politics."

"You learn a bit about outguessing opponents and calculating moves," McMaster said matter-of-factly.

Having tossed aside her book, Eleanor looked over the chessboard. "Please, Nick, show me how you did it," she said, smiling flirtatiously.

Stretching his arms after the concentration of the game, her brother remarked, "Eleanor has never in her life been interested in chess. You should consider this quite a triumph, Nick."

"I have, too!" Eleanor said, leaning down and tweaking his ear, while she smiled playfully at McMaster, showing the little gaps between her teeth. "At least, I might as well be interested in chess as anything else on a day as dull as this," she added.

McMaster sat back in his chair and studied her from behind his hooded eyes. "If I told you my secrets," he said, "you might pass them on, and, next thing, women could take over the world. Before we knew it, you'd be assemblymen, senators. Why, Miss Eleanor, you might even succeed Andrew Jackson as president of the Union."

Eleanor laughed delightedly over his nonsense, while Sam muttered, "As if it's not bad enough now, when she thinks she's a princess."

Frowning at her brother, Eleanor reached for his ear again, which he hastily covered with his hand. "It seems to me, Nick," Sam said with mock seriousness, "that Her Highness won't stop pestering us till you've shown her your ingenuity. Tell her what to do with herself."

One by one McMaster was putting chessmen back in their box. "I'm sure Miss Eleanor can think of something," he said. "After all, if she doesn't show her talent, we won't have her as president. Choose whatever you want, Miss Eleanor. I promise to be a loyal member of your constituency."

Eleanor smiled mischievously, pleased as always to be addressed with their guest's odd mixture of gallantry and formality. Affecting pensiveness, she walked back and forth in front of the window. "I know!" she exclaimed. "Let's go sleigh riding! If I don't get out and do something, I think I'll burst."

"Your idea of something to do would have to be chillblains and cold misery," drawled her brother.

"I never think of that," retorted Eleanor. "What you have to think about is ripping along behind a good horse, with the air crisp and the snow sparkling. Oh, that's heavenly!" she said, clapping her hands.

"Your idea of heaven is mine of total lunacy," countered Sam. "You can count on me staying right here beside the fire."

Pouting prettily, Eleanor turned to McMaster. "You see how Sam treats me," she said. "Oh, Nick, do say you feel like a sleigh ride! It's so much fun to trot along with all the ruts filled in and everything clean and pretty. You have to go! Besides, everybody will be out sleighing after a good snow, especially on Christmas Eve."

McMaster's eyelids lifted for a moment, giving an effect of intense concentration, before he stood up, bowed slightly, and said, "Since I've pledged myself, I'll go along, of course. What do I have to do to get ready?"

Eleanor caught his look and felt a moment of trepidation, as though what she'd impulsively arranged might turn out to be more than a simple evening of sleigh riding. "I'll see if Martha wants to go," she blurted, her face hot with a sudden blush. McMaster again bowed slightly. "—And whether Papa can spare the horse," she rushed on, "—and whether Gumbo and the men can get the sleigh ready. They might be too busy," she finished lamely.

"They finished digging out the lane a half hour ago," Sam drawled, "but I doubt that you'll budge Martha from that new book she's buried in. You may have noticed, Nick," he explained to his friend, "that unlike some people I could mention, my other sister's tastes run to serious reading. In fact, Martha pretty well divides her time between sermons and radicalism —when she's not running the Fox, that is."

Sam's comments gave Eleanor time to recover from her stab of hesitation. "Oh dear!" she exclaimed, glancing at the clock. "Look how late it is!" Again caught up in the excitement of her project, she hurried out of the room, ordering McMaster to be bundled up and ready and leaving Sam looking at the clock and chuckling.

Her first stop was the kitchen, where she commandeered Davy's services, leaving Catherine to wash her own pots and dishes. Eleanor didn't like to go into the common room of the inn, and her first order to Davy was to call her father from his wicket with word that she wanted to ask him something. When the Squire heard her plan, he growled that it was the kind of foolishness he might have expected and instantly ordered Davy to fetch Gumbo Jim from where he was still clearing snow in the courtyard. When Gumbo came in, tired and wet to the knees, the Squire ordered him out again to get the sleigh ready.

As soon as her father went back to the taproom, Eleanor announced to Catherine, "You can do that later. Be a dear for now and roast some chestnuts for us." As she breezed out of the kitchen she called back, "And don't forget to heat a bag of corn to keep our feet warm!"

Next Eleanor flew to the small upstairs room reserved for the women of the family. As she expected, she found her mother and sister there, Penelope Carpenter critically inspecting the latest mending by the hired girls, and Martha deep in another of the disagreeable-looking books she read in the odd times she wasn't working.

"Papa says we can take out the sleigh!" Eleanor exclaimed as she burst into the room.

Mrs. Carpenter put down the tablecloth she was frowning over and turned to her daughter. "As if your father ever once said no when you asked him for anything," she said. "I suppose you'll spend the whole night gallivanting from one place to another—and sleep so late you'll miss Christmas breakfast. I might have expected it."

"Don't be cross, Mama," Eleanor said. "Everybody will be out sleighing. Isn't it glorious that the snow came on Christmas Eve?"

Penelope Carpenter was more pleased than not to think of the brilliant effect her Passmore daughter would make visiting through the neighborhood, but as a point of policy, she opposed her husband's decisions, thus having the privilege of the last word if anything went wrong. Still, her point made, she turned to serious matters and asked what Eleanor was going to wear. "Since you'll be out in the cold, you'd better put on the grey merino," she said.

Eleanor wrinkled her nose. "Oh, Mama," she said, "I can't wear that drab thing on Christmas Eve. I thought I'd put on my green silk."

"—And no doubt the slippers to match," countered Mrs.

Carpenter, knowing full well that Eleanor would do whatever she wanted. "The grey is more appropriate—considering your situation," she added pointedly.

"I'm not married!" Eleanor protested, tears starting to her eyes, "And I'm not a widow, either, and I won't dress like one!"

Mrs. Carpenter shrugged. As usual, Martha hadn't been consulted. Now she looked up from her book and said quietly, "You can wear my velvet bonnet, if you want."

Startled, Eleanor said, "But Martha, I thought you'd come along. I thought we'd make a party of it."

"I have a notion we'll have parties enough right here, if everybody else has the same idea you have," Mrs. Carpenter retorted. "With Mrs. Belcher laid up with her holiday asthma, I can hardly spare Martha—though, of course she can go for an hour or two—if she wants to."

"Thank you, but I'd rather read," Martha said. "The three of you will get on well enough without me," she added wryly.

"But Sam says he won't come," Eleanor explained, feeling a strange mixture of dread and anticipation. "Mama, do you think it's all right for me to go out alone with Mr. McMaster?"

Mrs. Carpenter looked annoyed. "An American woman hardly needs a chaperone when she's with a friend of the family," she said, "though I must say, Eleanor, this is the first time I ever heard you fussing over proprieties."

"If you say so, Mama," Eleanor answered, giving her mother a peck on the cheek. She glanced at Martha's book just long enough to remark that it looked perfectly horrid, then hesitated. "Are you sure you won't come along, just for a bit?" she asked. Martha's decided no closed the door to that possibility, and Eleanor scurried from the room to get ready for sleigh riding.

Once settled beside McMaster, with a heavy blanket tucked over her legs and her feet warm against a sack of hot corn, Eleanor's misgivings gave way to exhilaration. Nothing was as wonderful as gliding over a snow-covered road, ordinary jolts and bruises magically transformed into a kind of dream. At first

Eleanor insisted on driving, but the horse was mettlesome after being penned in the stable, and her hands got cold. It was only minutes before McMaster took the reins.

They weren't alone, snowfall always calling out parties of young people, tonight, especially, making the most of the holiday. Bells jingled ahead and behind, signalling other sleighs, mostly hidden by rises and dips in the road. The ones they passed were filled with happy revellers, who waved and called out greetings.

At Eleanor's command, they drove east, while the light faded in the sky in front of them. When McMaster suggested they stop a few miles down the road, Eleanor exclaimed, "That's not a proper inn. Besides, I want to go as far as we can while I'm snug and warm! We can stop when we're cold, on the way back."

So they went on, across to the turnpike through a lane filled with drifts the horse struggled through, then on down the turnpike, now and again pausing to pay tolls but not stopping till they got to the banks of the Pequea. Only a red glow was left in the sky behind them by the time they pulled in and joined the crowd at the Spread Eagle.

"Let's keep on going," said Eleanor, when they came out again, and they drove farther east, stopping once more when they got as far as the John Adams, where McMaster jokingly remarked that a Jackson man might not be welcome. "A man like you is welcome anywhere," Eleanor breathed, and felt her arm tingle with an answering pressure from McMaster's hand. Warmed once more over the fire, the hot punch, and the crowd of boisterous holiday-makers, Eleanor felt reckless and light. "Let's keep on," she said, "Let's go all the way to Philadelphia!"

Startling her with the intensity of his gaze, McMaster smiled. "As your family's guest, I'm afraid I have to take you home," he said. "Even a princess has to be guided by her advisor."

"If he's a devoted one," Eleanor answered, studying him out of the corner of her eye.

"Devoted enough," McMaster replied.

Back in the sleigh, he finally turned the horse towards home. By now the moon had risen, its cold light reflecting from the snow and giving Eleanor the eerie feeling that the world she knew had turned inside out, the yellow light of day replaced by the silvery landscape of a dream or a fairy tale. Her green slippers were wet from the snow, and the bag of corn felt now like a pillow of ice spreading up through her body. She had the odd fancy that she was turning into an ice statue and might sit forever, throned on the seat of the sleigh and turn as translucent as the moonlight. "I won't be able to have a fire in my room," she thought irrationally, "and in the spring Papa will have to sit me on a block in the icehouse." Aloud, she said, "Let's go faster, Nick! I want to go fast!" McMaster slashed the horse's flank, and they flew towards the west.

They stopped twice more, McMaster each time fetching her a glass of hot punch, to make sure, he said, that she didn't turn into an ice princess. At last the Fox appeared, its walls black between the white ground and the snow on the roof. From the courtyard they could hear the noise of celebration from the taproom, while the shivering Gumbo took charge of their horse, muttering that they shouldn't have run him so hard in the cold.

McMaster swung Eleanor down from the sleigh, but to her surprise, she couldn't feel the ground. It flashed through her mind that her fancies during the ride were true. "I've turned into ice and moonlight," she thought, as McMaster held her from falling. He supported her as far as the steps, then swung her legs across his arm and carried her up, then again supported her through the house and upstairs as far as the door of her room. There he paused, his hand on the latch. "May I look in after a bit, to make sure you're all right?" he asked, staring into her eyes.

As though she were dreaming, Eleanor nodded. "I know I'll be all right now," she whispered, her head swirling.

8.

Catherine spent Christmas Eve bustling about the taproom and drawing mugs of beer and cider for thirsty holiday-makers, while the Squire, stationed at his grate, distributed the more potent of the Fox's offerings. Knots of young people appeared regularly, cheeks pink with cold and calling for mugs of cider or glasses of punch from the bowl the Squire replenished regularly and heated with a hiss and a cloud of steam from the loggerhead, on this occasion, when even women visited the taproom.

Other years, Catherine would have been sleighing with her friends. Minna and Aaron Denlinger would probably have stopped for her, and she and Minna would have crowded, giggling, on either side of Aaron, while he joked about having two girls to trade off and shook his head at the trouble of getting both of them off his hands before he could find one of his own to take home.

Besides the celebrating young people, the Fox also had its quota of regulars, like John Skiles and Tall Hen, sitting as usual on either end of the settee by the fire and studying each new knot of arrivals to keep up on which farmer's son was currently sweet on which farmer's daughter. When strange faces appeared, Skiles called Catherine over and quizzed her about who they were, or, failing that, intercepted the newcomers themselves to ask the names of their parents and the precise locations of their farms, not satisfied till he'd established the identity of uncles and aunts as well as two generations of grandparents.

"Cletus Fenstermacher," he was saying to one reluctant young man, while he scratched his head. "Now might that be the brother to the Phares Fenstermacher that had the farm over by Molasses Hill that had the sinkhole that someone fell into, onct?"

Without waiting for an answer, he turned to his crony, keeping the young man trapped till he finished. "You mind on that, Hen?" he asked across the bench. "I had it from my pap, and he had it from his, how the man that settled that place was ploughin' a field he'd just cleared along with his daughter, when the ground opened up under 'em. He let go the plough in time, but next thing he knowed, the ground just swallered up his ox and his plough and his girl and all. Nobody never seen her again," he added, shaking his jowls, "—or the plough neither, and he needed it and the ox, about then."

"I ain't no relation to that Fenstermacher," the young man said hastily, and escaped to fill his mug and chat with Catherine.

Tonight, especially, Catherine met lots of young people, because sleighers always stopped at inns, where a girl from one group might be second cousin to a young man from another and the link to yet another, while Catherine's friends from Stumptown and Mellinger's all greeted her and introduced her to their friends.

The young man whose uncle didn't live at Molasses Hill was especially taken with Catherine and followed her around, offering to help her and asking questions about her family and, especially, her father's farm. "Ach, now," she finally said, laughing and speaking in German, like most of the other young people, "you're underfoot like a mess of kittens, and I got work to do. You'd better look sharp," she added mischievously, "or you won't get a girl to take home." Reluctantly, the young man went back to a group in the corner, where he continued to follow Catherine with soulful eyes.

The taproom swirled with movement, as young people came and went, calling out alternate greetings and goodbyes. Trying to keep up with the calls to her in between, Catherine was drawing more cider, when someone boomed in German, "Where's that serving girl when somebody wants her?" Catherine stiffened, suddenly self-conscious as she recognized Jake Good's voice.

He was laughing, as usual, and his unruly red hair made him look taller by a head than any other man in the room. With a glance, Catherine took in that tonight he wasn't dressed like a wagoner. He'd left behind his cowhide coat and was wearing respectable homespun like the rest of the young men, who greeted him merrily as he walked in. "We'll have a night of it now!" said one. "Jake'll stay till the Squire outens the lights and the beer gets all!"

Catherine was flustered by his arrival. Grateful as she was for being rescued from the snake, she was still offended by Jake's loudness and his marked attention to her, which he flaunted for everyone to see. As a result, she was always acutely aware when he was at the Fox, which was quite often, she thought, considering that his father's farm was a good distance down the road towards Philadelphia, where he delivered freight from barges at Columbia and exchanged them for goods to be shipped west.

If Catherine hadn't seen him arrive or, by some miracle, he was less loud than usual, she always knew he was around from the way Gumbo Jim laughed and chuckled. And Jake was certainly a favorite with Mrs. Belcher, who shook with laughter at his teasing and wheezed that he should have met her when she was only a slip of a girl. But Catherine was surprised at Jim, who seemed to think that next to Davy, Jake Good was his best friend.

The redheaded wagoner, after all, was only a farm boy of the sort Catherine had grown up with, and he had a few redeeming traits. Although he had a tremendous thirst, he quenched it only with small beer, never anything stronger, she had to admit, and he never was the least bit tipsy. And she knew by now that beer hadn't any more effect than water on the booming of Jake's voice or the extravagance of his humor.

She had to admit, too, that he was a good worker, though for him wagoning was only winter work. His outfit was small, but it was spruce and handsome, with graceful ironwork crafted by his uncle, and his horses were well-fed and pampered, each one stepping proudly under its arch of bells. All four were invariably groomed and fed before Jake set foot in the taproom. And she knew firsthand how skillful he was with the whip, which good drivers used only to play over their horses' ears and signal them what to do next.

Thinking of Jake's handiness with the whip made Catherine blush, reminding her again of the neat job he'd made of patching the fireplace so that she wouldn't have to worry again about snakes. Blushing more deeply, she also remembered Mrs. Belcher's sly wheeze, "Somebody's sweet on somebody."

Answering a deep shout from across the room, Catherine drew three mugs of beer, pausing as she carried them over to mark them next to Jake Good's name on the tally slate.

"I'm sure glad somebody else is minding my P's and Q's for me," Jake announced to general laughter as she put them on a table. "I'd sure hate to have to do it all by myself." To Catherine's surprise, he turned back to talk with his friends, leaving her nonplussed and surprisingly disappointed.

But she hadn't time to brood about Jake's change to her, because Catherine had never been busier since she came to the Fox. She'd been hired to work in the kitchen, where Martha Carpenter was currently minding the fire, not to wait in the taproom and do Mrs. Belcher's job. In fact, she couldn't help wondering if Mrs. Belcher really was lying in bed and wheezing with asthma or whether she might not be taking the chance to enjoy Christmas with her family—as Catherine heartily wished she were doing too. Hastily, she pushed aside such an uncharitable thought.

She was drawing more cider when a familiar voice spoke over her shoulder. "Katlie," her father said, "I brought somebody to see you." Catherine wheeled around, while her brother Peter dived past her in time to close the cider bung, greeting her as he straightened up.

Although she'd been home every other Sunday, Peter hadn't been, and she'd seen him only at church, thanks to his apprenticeship with Adam Wenger. Catherine surveyed her younger brother and decided that he looked well and happy. It might have been a trick of her eyes, but Peter looked less childish than he had a month ago. "I'm making spokes now, and Adam Wenger's teaching me how to set them in the wheels," he said proudly.

"I talked to Adam at church, and he gave Peter Christmas home," Gideon explained to Catherine. "We went out hunting today and got a buck we just brought over to the Squire's."

Uneasily, Catherine remembered her father's need for money and knew that he and Peter hadn't been hunting to stock the family larder. "I have to serve this cider," she said, wishing her father and brother had shown up any other evening of the year except now, this busiest of all times, when she couldn't even talk to them.

"You go on about your business," Gideon said. "We'll make do and look after ourselves—but first, draw us a couple mugs."

Catherine obliged before scurrying off to look after the company, while Gideon and Peter moved about chatting with friends and exchanging news.

Busy as she was, it was half an hour before she could speak to them again. To her surprise, her father was sitting with Jake Good and in the middle of a serious conversation. As she approached, she heard Jake say to her father, "So you see, there ain't much chance of it unless you got your own wagon and a good team of Conestogas."

With a sinking heart, Catherine realized that her father was talking with the redheaded wagoner about another way of raising money, this one futile, because they had only two horses on the farm and used cattle for most heavy work.

"How'd you get set up?" Gideon asked, still engrossed in the conversation.

"My uncle had a penny put by and backed me," Jake answered. "I got him paid off a year or two back, so now I can save up what I make." Gideon nodded, assuming that the young man intended to buy a farm of his own as soon as he could.

Both of them ignored Catherine, who stood waiting till her father was ready to notice her. But Gideon wasn't in a hurry to end the conversation. Instead, he followed up on the young man's future plans, apparently liking Jake and curious to know how close he was to buying a farm of his own. "You got a girl picked out yet?" Gideon asked.

"I got my eye on one," Jake answered, looking at Gideon but watching Catherine out of the corner of his eye, "one that knows how to cook, anyhow."

Catherine's ears burned. The impudent rascal meant her, she thought angrily. She decided she'd heard enough. Doing her best to ignore Jake Good, she broke in to tell her father that she'd be home for an hour or two tomorrow after dinner. Gideon nodded, replying simply that her mother would be looking for her. With an indignant glance at Jake Good, Catherine hurried off to more chores, and Gideon shook hands with Jake, called Peter, and slipped out the door.

As the evening wore on, swirling knots of young people formed and reformed before gradually thinning out. Replacing mugs on the rack, Catherine was suddenly all ears as she heard Jake Good's voice sounding among the goodbyes. She turned in time to see him at the door with a pretty, dark-haired young woman he was obviously about to take home. This must be the girl who knew how to cook, Catherine realized, her heart suddenly sinking.

9.

Congress was back in session, awaiting the arrival of the new president, and the State Assembly was back in Harrisburg, passing legislation and steering the course of the Commonwealth. The holiday season had passed as completely as Mrs. Belcher's asthma attack (which Gumbo Jim confidently predicted would recur at Easter). Mrs. Belcher's return to the taproom lightened Catherine's work, but she was more and more uneasy at being away from home.

On the Sundays she spent with her family and the occasional hours she snatched from her work to look in on them, Catherine was more and more worried about her mother. From one visit to the next, Catherine thought, Elizabeth looked more tired. Moreover, her movements were slower than they used to be, as though even ordinary chores needed a special effort to finish. Most surprising, she was now and then sharp with the boys. She'd always been firm when she corrected them, but now her voice sometimes had an irritable edge when she reprimanded them for ordinary shrieks and squabbles. Her cough persisted, but Catherine was old enough to suspect that something more was affecting her mother's health.

They were alone, washing dishes on one of Catherine's Sundays at home, when Elizabeth suddenly gasped and dropped a dish. "What's wrong, Mama?" Catherine exclaimed, hurriedly wiping her hands and helping her mother to a chair.

"It ain't nothing," Elizabeth murmured. "I'll be myself in a minute." She sat bolt upright swallowing air. After a minute or so, she stood up. "It's no good," she said. "I got to go to the outhouse."

By the time she got back, Catherine was putting the last of the dishes back in the cupboard. "Mama," Catherine said, sitting down beside Elizabeth at the table, "how long have you been like this?"

"Ach, Katlie, I can't hardly say anymore," Elizabeth said wearily. "Seems like I ain't been right since summer, only it's worse now."

"Does Pap know?" Catherine asked.

"Not the whole of it," Elizabeth answered reluctantly. "Your pap has enough on his plate just now, without my giving him more worry." She reached over and squeezed her daughter's hand. "I'm glad you're home, Katlie. There's things a woman don't talk to her man about."

Catherine waited, knowing how hard it was for Elizabeth to talk about female complaints, even normal ones. "It's a new baby, ain't?" she finally prompted.

Elizabeth nodded. "I thought maybe you'd guessed already." She looked at her daughter with worried eyes, a frown puckering the top of her nose. "Problem is, this baby ain't like the other ones, I can tell. Benny wasn't easy, but I never got this sick. This time I can't even hold down my dinner, and it's all I can do to put your Pap's food on the table, the smell of it greisels me so."

Very worried now, Catherine asked what doctoring she'd been doing for it.

"Lena Groff told me to take barley water and sugar, and that settles me some. But that ain't really what ails me," Elizabeth added. "I tell you, Katlie," she said, lowering her voice, "this baby ain't right. I think it got marked."

Catherine gasped. Everyone in the neighborhood knew about the little boy with the birthmark over half his face and why he was born with it, after his mother scalded her hand and then held it against her face. "What happened to you, Mama?" Catherine asked, horrified.

"I didn't tell nobody when it happened," Elizabeth said, dropping her voice. "I'd taken some potpie over to Lena Groff. —You mind when she was ailing, and I knew she'd want something besides her daughter-in-law's cooking. Anyhow, it was almost dark till I got started home. I'd got as far as the fencerow where your pap's land starts, when something rose up in front of me. It looked like it came straight out of the ground, and I saw eyes shining at me. Then it stood up till it got taller than I was, and I tell you, Katlie, it was black as pitch!"

Catherine stared, tongue-tied, and Elizabeth concluded, "I ain't been right since, or the baby either."

The two sat in silence, Elizabeth lost in foreboding, and Catherine wondering and looking for words to comfort her. "Don't say nothing to your pap," her mother admonished, as foot stamping signalled the return of Gideon and the boys.

Catherine wouldn't betray a confidence, but she decided that she had to share her more general worries with Gideon, in the meantime doing all she could to lighten Elizabeth's work. As soon as she had the chance, she followed her father to the barn, and scrambled up the ladder behind him when he climbed upstairs to pitch down bedding for the livestock. While she waited for him to finish, Catherine studied the lines etched into his face and realized that it had been months since she'd heard him teasing the boys with German riddles or telling droll stories about his encounters with John Skiles.

As he hung up the fork and started towards the ladder, Catherine stopped him. "Pap, I've been wanting to ask how long you want me to stay at the Fox," she said, "and when I can move back home."

Gideon turned slowly, as if he'd been half expecting the question. "It may be a while yet," he said, "though I wish I could say different. We'd best talk," he added.

Catherine hoisted herself onto a wagon stored between the mows, and Gideon joined her. When he spoke, his voice was low, and he began with a question. "Has Mrs. Carpenter said anything yet on raising your pay, the way she said she would?"

Catherine shook her head. Father and daughter both knew how stingy the mistress of the Fox was, a fact as notorious as Patience Slack's taste for drink. "I'll see what I can do to jiggle her memory," Gideon said.

Screwing up her courage, Catherine said, "I think Mama could do with some help," watching her father's face.

"Your mama's been ailing since summer," Gideon said slowly, "and now she's worse than she is better. I know it, though she don't say much." Instead of looking at her, he was staring at the bars of light coming in from the slits beyond the haymow. "Every day now, I half expect she'll take to her bed, but she keeps going. And that's what we all got to do," he concluded.

Catherine knew better than to question or contradict, but her worry over her mother got the better of her. "If I was home, I could lighten things for her," she said eagerly.

Gideon frowned and shook his head. "We can't spare the money you're bringing in," he said, with an edge of bitterness. He tore his eyes from the light shafts to glance at his daughter. "Owen Rees wants his pay. I can't fault a man for wanting the money he worked for," he added, "but it puts me in a bind."

If only from John Skiles's regular broadcasts of everybody else's business, Catherine knew that her father wouldn't get paid for his land till Squire Carpenter found one of the Wilson brothers, lost somewhere in Kentucky, but she hadn't heard about the quarry. "I thought you and Mr. Rees had a bargain worked out," she said.

Gideon smiled grimly. "So did I," he answered, "and he did

too. Rees said he'd take out a good part of it in stone for a house he's putting up down the road for Elam Fisher." His eyes were fixed on the bars of light, and Catherine waited, dreading what he'd say next.

"That was till last week, when a man from Lancaster showed up with a paper in English. You recollect when I was at the Fox last," Gideon reminded his daughter. She remembered well enough that her father had disappeared upstairs to see the Squire in his office. "There's been a mistake in a boundary line. And the upshot is," Gideon concluded, "the law says the quarry ain't ours."

Catherine exploded with indignation. "That can't be!" she exclaimed. "It was measured. I remember those men coming out and doing it with their chains when you sold that piece off to Miles Wilson!"

"We all thought so," Gideon said wearily, "and Wilson did too. Only, some lawyers in Lancaster got to checking out old papers, and they say the line got shifted five hundred yards or so from where it was when the land got divided. They say the piece I sold Wilson has to be measured from the first line. And that takes in the quarry, too," he concluded.

"You can't let them get away with it!" Catherine said angrily. "If they can hire lawyers to say black is white, why can't you get one of your own and fight them?"

"The Squire says the law's the law," Gideon answered. He looked at his daughter appraisingly. "Remember, Katlie," he pronounced in a voice she was more used to hearing in church than in the barn, "our way is to follow the law, not to fight it."

He sighed, then stood up and headed for the stable ladder. Catherine started to follow, when Gideon turned back. "One more thing, Katlie. Don't say nothing to your mother. It's enough that I got to lay part of my burden on you, but she's not strong enough now to bear more than she has to." He wheeled and disappeared down the ladder.

As Catherine walked back to the house, she felt years older than she had yesterday. Passing the new building, she stopped to look into one of the holes waiting for sash and glazing before it could turn into a window. Flooring hid the cellar, but the outlines of what were to be the upper stories were only beams, skeletal and black in the chilly light from the open roof. Catherine shivered and hurried towards the kitchen.

10.

Gideon indeed jiggled Mrs. Carpenter's memory about her promise to raise Catherine's pay, which, the lady insisted, had been provisional, not a solid commitment. She stood by her bargain only after Gideon pointed out that with Catherine's experience now, she could find work someplace else. Luckily, the day Gideon saw the mistress of the Fox, she'd had a previous visitor.

Patience Slack had lasted less than three weeks at the Bird-in-Hand and hardly longer at the Drover, where she'd been a greater favorite with the clientele than with Mick Clancy, the proprietor. Carpetbag once more in hand, she was trudging down the road again, this time in the opposite direction.

"If you please, Missus," she told Mrs. Carpenter, "I'm a changed woman since I was here. I've give up the drink. I ain't had a drop in ten days." Her breath, however, told a different story, and in short order she was back on the road heading towards Lancaster. Still, her visit gave Mrs. Carpenter a view of life at the Fox if Catherine left.

Eleanor Johns fluttered about in high good spirits, ecstatic over Nicholas McMaster's promise to see her divorce through the State Assembly and at the prospect of seeing him when he came back to Lancaster for the Birthday Ball. Gigues and gavottes tinkled through the upstairs of the inn whenever Eleanor got bored with whatever else she was doing, like painting flowers on tea cups or embroidering handkerchiefs, while Martha and her mother went about the business of running the inn.

The Squire was in good spirits, too, his growl not quite a purr, but his bark erupting less often than usual. Sam's tip about the route for the railroad had been confirmed, and from Will Carpenter's perspective, it came at exactly the right time, thanks to his role as Miles Wilson's executor. The brother in Kentucky hadn't been found yet, and, till he was, the Squire had full power to manage Wilson's property, even (unofficially) to dip into the principal and clear a mortgage on the Fox he'd inherited along with the business and property. Thanks to prudent management, the debt had dwindled, but now the Fox was free of it. Eventually the money would have to be paid back, but not till the misplaced brother emerged from the far Kentucky hills.

And prospects for paying the money back looked bright, because the Squire had arranged to lease the land Gideon Landis had sold Wilson. Thanks to Sam's porings over dusty maps, that parcel now included a fine quarry full of rock hard enough to bed the tracks for the railroad.

But if the Squire and his daughter were happy, their mood hadn't spread to the lower parts of the inn. Catherine was jumpy and irritable, her mother's health constantly on her mind. She was so preoccupied that she barely noticed that Gumbo Jim was depressed, too, till one day Davy asked why everyone was so grumpy. Startled, Catherine asked him what he was talking about.

"Well, you're always grumpy now," Davy said, "and Gumbo don't even talk to me no more. He grouses all the time, and he won't hardly let me help him with the horses. And that ain't like Gumbo. Like you, either," he added.

Catherine felt stabs of guilt, since Davy's life was hard enough without her making it worse. She felt especially bad that Davy was being snubbed by the one person at the Fox he admired. Jim had a special way, a magic even, with horses, and Davy dogged his heels every moment he could sneak away from the kitchen and taproom. "Seems like all he does nowadays is stand around and stare at that dumb eagle," Davy said glumly.

Feeding the chained eagle was one of Gumbo's jobs. The Squire had picked it up a few years back, after some boys found it with a broken wing and offered it to him for a few cents. By now its wing was long healed, and it had become a fixture, huddling in its lean-to against the carriage shed and glaring at the children who walked to the Fox to see it and poke it with sticks when Gumbo wasn't by to stop them.

Because of Davy, Catherine decided to talk to Jim, though she didn't have a chance till she'd finished Tuesday baking and went looking for him, a half-moon pie in hand.

She found him in the stable grooming the Squire's favorite horse, a Narragansett Pacer Jim took special pride in after doctoring him over a lame foot. Catherine waited while Jim ate the pie and wiped his mouth. "Are you mad at Davy?" she asked then.

Jim went back to currying the horse, sweeping him with firm, gentle strokes. Finally, he said, "No, Missy, I ain't mad at nobody, least at nobody round here."

Turning over a bucket, Catherine sat down in a corner of the stall, determined to get to the bottom of Jim's bad humor. "Well, Davy sure thinks you are," she said. "All he talks about is what happened so you don't like him. He thinks he must of done something."

"That poor child ain't never done nothing, except get underfoot trying to help me," Jim responded. "What's he think that for?"

"He just does," Catherine said, "mostly because he says you don't talk to him now, when you used to be his best friend."

"Sometimes a load's too heavy for someone little as Davy is," Gumbo drawled, and walked to the other side of the horse, where he studied Catherine over the Pacer's back. He watched her a bit. Finally he said, "You remember me telling you once about my brother?"

Catherine shuddered, remembering Gumbo's silent description of what his brother would do if he was sold to a rice plantation. "He ain't done it!" she cried.

"No, Missy," Gumbo said quietly. "He ain't cut his hand off, leastways not yet, only maybe worse. Cassius, he run off." Catherine stared at Gumbo, who added, "Now what you think of that?"

Catherine shook her head, but Gumbo watched her, waiting to know what she really did think about it. "I think he's in trouble," she said finally. "And, Jim, I sure hope he don't get caught!"

"Maybe he will, and maybe he won't," Gumbo said philosophically. "Only thing I know for sure is, Cassius get this far, he's going to make a visit. But if the Squire catch him here, he'll say, 'That's prime livestock on the hoof, and it belongs to somebody.' Then, Squire, he'll pack Cassius up and send him back to Virginia."

Catherine nodded gloomily, knowing Gumbo was right. And she realized why Gumbo was telling her about it. "I'll help if I can," she said slowly.

Gumbo smiled and went back to grooming the horse.

Because of her talk with Gumbo, Catherine wasn't caught completely off guard when the crisis he predicted developed a few weeks later. She was taking supper off the fire when Jim came in from the stables. Before he sat down, he stood beside her a few moments at the fireplace and flexed his hands in the heat. Looking over his shoulder to be sure Davy wouldn't hear, he whispered, "Missy, can you slip me any extra food when I go back out?" He didn't meet her eyes and added, "Best not ask questions, only I'm real hungry tonight, maybe tomorrow, too." When they finished eating, Jim carried bread and a joint of meat along back to the stable.

Catherine was nervous all the next day. Farm families ate early, but supper wasn't served at the Fox till seven, giving her time in the afternoon to get ready for Friday baking in the spring house. Everyone used the outdoor steps, though a narrow ladder under a trap door led down to the spring and a store of lard, milk, and butter. Another ladder led to the loft, where dried fruit and vegetables hung in bags from the rafters and a smokehouse filled the corner by the chimney. Bins of rye and wheat flour lined one wall of the room where Catherine worked, handy to the dough tray and the table where she rolled out pastry.

Eleanor Johns fluttered in, and Catherine set her to stirring a pot of apple snitz, while she kneaded lard into a mess of flour and sugar for the shoofly pies she'd finish in the morning. Eleanor had been more effervescent than usual in the last month and hadn't once stared into the fire or mentioned the little boy she didn't have. Instead, she'd bubbled on happily and incessantly about one thing or another, always ending by talking about Nicholas McMaster and prodding Catherine to praise him.

Catherine couldn't. She disliked McMaster and shivered when she remembered first seeing him. So she evaded Eleanor, usually asking some question to send her flying off in a new direction. Today Catherine turned her by asking what she'd heard about her divorce.

Eleanor beamed. "Nick wrote Sam that he'll put it through next month. Oh, Catherine!" she burst out, in her thin, clear voice. "Nick's so different from Alec. If only you knew!" Catherine waited for some explanation, but, as usual, didn't get any. Instead, forgetting kettle and spoon, Eleanor danced from the fireplace, exclaiming, "I can't believe that I'll really be free! — not have to keep out of sight unless Alec wants to show me off for company, not have to sit down at the piano the minute he says, 'Eleanor plays so beautifully.' Catherine, you don't know what freedom means!"

Meanwhile, Catherine hurried to the fireplace, stirred the kettle, and lifted it from the fire. "Seems to me nobody is free, when things got to be looked after," she said. "Something or other is likely to get scorched."

It was getting dark, a sign to finish up and go back to the kitchen, when Catherine heard a hubbub in the courtyard. Looking out the window, she noticed a parked wagon, which, from the size and the bow of the body, she knew was Jake Good's. She looked to see if Jake was in sight, but instead saw the Squire arguing loudly with two strangers. Remembering Jim's brother, she opened the window a crack to hear what they were saying, Eleanor at her side, as curious as she was to know what the Squire was shouting about.

"I tell you, I don't know nothing about none of your runaways," he was thundering, "and you've no call to search my place! You want somebody that hides another man's property, you go down the road to Enterprise and look in Dan Gibbons' barns, not mine!"

The other men spoke more quietly, and Catherine strained to catch fragments of what they were saying. The Squire, too, dropped to a milder register. While Catherine and Eleanor watched in the half-light, he turned abruptly and led the strange men towards the stable.

"Who are those men?" Eleanor asked, as steps sounded on the stairs. Without answering, Catherine closed the window, just as Martha Carpenter opened the door, on one of her rounds to check on Catherine's work.

"Oh, Martha!" Eleanor exclaimed, as Catherine hurried to cover pots and basins. "Do you know who those men are?"

Unlike her sister, Martha Carpenter never showed her feelings. She answered curtly, "They're slavers from Virginia, looking for a runaway."

"How horrid!" Eleanor exclaimed, while Catherine's heart sank. "How can they think anyone here would hide a slave?"

Eleanor added indignantly. "Papa would never stand for it."

"Could be Papa doesn't know about it," Martha answered, moving to the window and scrutinizing the courtyard, where voices indicated that Squire Carpenter and the searchers were leaving the stable.

"Have they found him?" Catherine breathed, stretching to see over Martha's shoulder.

"No," Martha answered, glancing at her sharply, "but they're sure to look everywhere. This place is probably next, then the barn."

The three stood listening, when Eleanor suddenly gave a little scream and pointed at the door to the spring room. "It's a rat!" she cried, as Catherine and Martha, too, heard scratching.

"Don't be a fool," Martha flashed out. She hurried to the trap door, tugged at the ring, and heaved it open.

Catherine felt a rush of cold from the hole at their feet. Looking up from it was a black man, whom Catherine guessed to be Jim's brother Cassius. Gumbo must have sent him to the spring house when the slavers searched the stable, trusting that she'd help and thinking she was alone. She felt paralyzed by bad luck, that Martha Carpenter had chosen this, of all times, to check on her. It flashed through her mind that she could have managed Eleanor, but Martha was her father's daughter, and she was sure to turn in Jim's brother.

Martha's face was impassive as she stared down at the black man and ordered, "Get up here, quick!"

Cassius scrambled up the ladder, stumbling onto his hands and knees as he climbed into the room. Still holding the ring, Martha gestured to Catherine. "Help me to shut it again. Don't let it bang," she added, as Catherine hurried to help, while the Negro rose to his feet. He watched them warily, while Martha continued, "They'll look down below first. We've got to think where to hide him."

As, together, they carefully shut the trap door, Catherine felt a new respect for Martha Carpenter and shame that she'd automatically judged her by her parents, as if people weren't responsible for themselves.

In their excitement, both of them forgot Eleanor. Shrinking from the black man as if he were a visitor from Tophet, Eleanor stood with her hand on the door latch. "I'll call Papa and the men!" she exclaimed, as Catherine and Martha simultaneously looked up.

But before Eleanor could open the door, Martha turned on her. "If you open that door, I'll make your life so miserable you'll wish you'd never been born," she said grimly. "You've never thought of anything but yourself in your whole life, and now you're ready to throw this man's life away. For just once, think what you're doing!"

Eleanor looked from Martha to Catherine and back in bewilderment. "But he's a runaway," she said. "He doesn't belong to us."

"Why should he belong to anybody?" Martha shot back. "You mark my words: one peep out of you when they get here, and I'll tell Papa some things I noticed over the holidays, about some late night visiting between you and a certain fancy politician." Eleanor gave a start, and Martha added, "Don't think I won't, too. Now, get out of the way. And remember, not one word!" Looking white and shaken, Eleanor moved from the door, as Martha turned to Cassius. "Has anyone seen you?"

"No'm," the black man answered in a drawl Catherine strained to understand. "Only one knows is Jimmy, and he's own brother to me."

Without commenting, Martha Carpenter turned to Catherine, as voices rose from the spring room. "We've got to think where to put him before they get here," she whispered. "The loft won't do," she added, following Catherine's glance. "They're sure to look there."

Catherine felt as if her brain had stopped. She darted looks around the room, hesitating as her eyes rested first on the bins of flour and finally on the chimney. Irrationally, she remembered Gumbo's ambition to be a chimney sweep and his ironic remark that soot doesn't show on a black man.

81

Following her glance, Martha shook her head. "That won't do. It's the first place they'll look," she said.

By now a door slammed downstairs and voices sounded outside. "They're taking the steps," Martha whispered. "Quick!" She ran to the trap door, Catherine beside her, and they heaved it back open. Lithely, Gumbo's brother swung himself onto the steps. "Stay there till we tell you," Martha commanded, as they lowered the door.

Catherine's last view of Cassius was the light reflecting from his eyes and black skin in the pit at her feet. They'd barely eased down the door and rushed to the work table, when the room shook from steps on the stairs, and the door opened.

"You'll see soon enough that there ain't no runaway here, neither," the Squire said gruffly, as the two strange men strode into the room.

"Maybe, maybe not," one of them answered. He paused when he saw the women and made a perfunctory bow. "Excuse us, ladies," he said with exaggerated politeness. "We got us some business to look to." His eyes swept the room. Without hesitating, he stepped to the fireplace, raised his lantern, and peered up the chimney, at the same time saying to his companion, "Hank, check them flour bins, 'case some niggah thinks runnin' off's turned him into a white man."

The second man took a poker from the fireplace and dug around the flour bins, while Catherine watched resentfully. "Ain't nothin' here," he reported.

The first one raised the lantern in the dying light and swept it around the room. "While we're here, we'll thank you just to let us look into that loft up there," he said to the Squire.

Muttering that they'd find as much up there as they had every place else, the Squire gestured them to look where they wanted and planted himself in front of the fireplace, legs apart and jaw thrust forward, glowering. Shortly, the tramping overhead was interrupted by the first man's demand for the key to the smokehouse, which the Squire thrust at him with an oath.

The visitors made their way back down the ladder, the Squire rumbling that he'd told them they were wasting their time but figured they wouldn't be satisfied till they'd nosed through his barn, upset his customers, and sampled his wine cellar, which, he muttered, they'd pay for through the nose. He wheeled and stomped to the door, which he nonetheless held open for the Southerners, and, for the first time, looked at the women.

"You must of been mighty busy out here," he growled, "if it takes all three of you to do the redding up."

"We're almost done," Martha said, and turned back as if to check Catherine's preparations. The Squire paused, then shut the door and followed the slave hunters down the steps.

As soon as they were gone, Eleanor laughed shrilly. "Papa will find out what you did," she said. "They'll find that slave the minute someone goes to fetch milk or butter, and we'll all get the blame."

Her sister looked at her coldly. "No one will find out unless you tell," she retorted, "and I've already told you what I'll do then. She's right, though," Martha said, turning to Catherine. "He can't stay there. Someone's bound to go in, most likely my father checking things before bed. We have to think of some place else for the night."

Still half thinking of the fireplace, Catherine said suddenly, "What about the bake oven? Davy didn't stoke it yet for the baking, and there's room enough inside, if he can squeeze in. I saw my pap crawl inside once when ours needed fixed."

"It may do," Martha said slowly. In a minute or two they decided that she and Eleanor would go right to the house and Catherine would look after Cassius. The three went out together, Martha and Eleanor to the kitchen and Catherine to the spring room, as if she had to collect supplies for supper. By now the slavers were out of sight, probably in the barn, but, at any rate, not likely to see another shadow in this light.

At first Catherine could only hear the gurgling of water against crocks of milk, but when she called softly, a dark figure stepped from behind the open door. She almost screamed but forced herself to speak slowly and explain the plan. Finally, she slipped towards the bake oven, Gumbo's brother behind her like an untimely shadow.

Showing him what he had to do, she apologized that he'd get dirty, but Cassius grinned, his teeth flashing in the dark. "Dirt don't always stick on them that's used to it," he said, thanked her, and, shoulders first, slowly squeezed into the oven.

Catherine watched as he disappeared and finally pulled in legs and feet. Then she whispered through the door, "You got room enough in there?"

A voice drawled back from the hollow dome, "It's like bein' back in my mammy's belly. It'll do."

Hurriedly, Catherine piled in a few sticks of wood to block the passage and was pushing the door to, when a voice beside her said in German, "You always work in the dark, yet?"

Catherine started. The light had all but failed, but she didn't need it to recognize Jake Good.

"I got baking to do tomorrow," she said, wondering how much he'd seen.

"That wood enough to fire it?" Jake asked. "Come on, I'll load it up so you can get an early start."

"It's late now," Catherine said, tugging at his arm as he made for the woodpile. "Davy'll do it in the morning," she added urgently. "And I got to get to the kitchen!"

"If you're inside or out, I can do it," Jake said. Dark as it was, Catherine knew he was grinning, and her temper flared. She remembered the last she'd seen of him, leaving the Fox with the pretty brunette, his flirting with her forgotten, while she watched and was humiliated that even for a minute she'd thought Jake Good was the least bit attractive.

"I wouldn't take help from you for anything in the world!" she exclaimed angrily. "Just knowing you touched the oven would turn pies sour. Now I got work to do," she finished, and headed for the kitchen.

"Wait up!" Jake called, his voice suddenly serious. "I was funning. There's something else." Jake hurried after her and said in her ear, "Gumbo sent me."

Catherine stopped. Considering the usual volume of his voice, Jake said very softly, "I got to know where Cassius is so I can get him out of here. Is it the oven?"

Catherine didn't know how to lie, but Jake was more likely than not to look for himself and find Cassius anyway, in spite of anything she could say.

"I told Gumbo I'd help," Jake added urgently, "but I can't without I know where he is. He's in the oven, ain't?"

"Please, Jake, don't tell nobody but Gumbo!" Catherine pleaded, nodding.

"Don't worry," he answered, touching her shoulder. "I'll see to it." Remarkably, Catherine was sure he would. She stood for a moment, hesitating, then hurried back to the kitchen to make supper.

11.

Eleanor Johns wasn't heartless, but she was badly spoiled. By Passmore standards, her mother had been fairly strict, at least in teaching her daughter how to be a lady. As a result, Eleanor knew the art of dressing becomingly and attracting any man within eyeing distance (as was appropriate for the flower of the Passmores), not at all like Martha, who turned a deaf ear to her mother's social lessons.

Still, Penelope Carpenter's influence was less important than the Squire's. Having married into a prominent, if not especially wealthy family, Will Carpenter fully intended his house to rise to new heights, and his pretty little girl had a central place in his blueprint. As a result, he'd indulged Eleanor's every whim, as proper to the daughter destined to raise higher still the fortunes of the house of Carpenter.

Eleanor had suffered during her marriage, especially when she lost her baby, but she knew that even princesses sometimes have trials before the prince finds them and sees that they live happily ever after. In all, she saw no reason to think that the world didn't revolve around her or to be concerned with anyone else's problems, like Catherine's worries about her family or Gumbo Jim's cold, caught tending her horse in a snowstorm. Certainly, the last person in the world she had any sympathy for was a black slave, who should have known his place and stayed there.

Nevertheless, Eleanor held her tongue about what happened in the spring house, partly because she was afraid of Martha, partly because the black man wasn't found in the morning, having disappeared as completely as the freight wagon parked behind the inn the night before. Besides, Eleanor had other matters to think of.

Through January and half of February she waited for word about her divorce, pestering Sam for news whenever he visited the Fox. Alec Johns had sent him a stiffly worded note agreeing not to oppose the proceedings, Sam's veiled threats having overweighed Johns's fear of social impropriety. What remained was merely for Nicholas McMaster to see Eleanor's divorce bill through the State Assembly.

Eleanor didn't doubt for a moment that McMaster would sweep away her problems and be her personal Prince Charming, though Catherine, the audience for her castle-building, had reservations. Unlike Eleanor, Catherine hadn't read much besides the Bible and the *Martyrs Mirror*, and wasn't used to fairy tales. But her views didn't matter, since Eleanor didn't listen to them anyway.

In the third week of February, word finally arrived that the divorce had passed, at the end of an especially long afternoon of petty business, when the few assemblymen who hadn't gone home were asleep in their chairs. Sam rode out from Lancaster with the news, but because he had business to look after, stayed just long enough to consult with his father about a contract with the railroad company and make arrangements for Saturday, when he was escorting Eleanor and his mother to the Birthday Ball.

If the Father of his Country wasn't invariably first in the hearts of all his countrymen, his birthday was the only chance for celebrating between Christmas and Easter. Most of the better people in and around Lancaster (whose husbands or sons were Masons) went to the ball in his honor, but because of her daughter's dubious marital position, Penelope Carpenter had misgivings when Eleanor announced that she intended to go.

Nicholas McMaster had managed the divorce admirably, even arranging to keep it out of the public record, where anyone could see it—at least anyone interested enough to check on how the State Assembly used public time and money. Penelope Carpenter didn't want publicity about a divorce and didn't tell even relatives, except, of course, her sister.

The minute McMaster's news arrived, a letter went off to Sophia Passmore, in discreetly veiled language. The letter also expressed reservations about Eleanor's new position as a divorcee, but when her mother mentioned them to the party in question, Eleanor tossed her head and insisted that no matter what anyone thought, she was going to the Birthday Ball. As usual, she got her way.

A sneezing Gumbo Jim delivered mother and daughter at Sam's rooms, where Eleanor feverishly checked to be sure her curls were in place and the flounces on her green silk dress in order, ignoring her mother's comment that she might more appropriately be wearing grey or black. Then the three set off down King Street towards the city square, Eleanor chattering non-stop about who they'd see and what they'd be wearing, her mind on a different subject. During his Christmas visit McMaster had mentioned that he'd be in Lancaster for the Birthday Ball, and Eleanor had no doubt that he was watching for her as eagerly as she was for him.

"For heaven's sake, Eleanor," Mrs. Carpenter admonished her as they reached the square. "I've never heard such babble. Anyone would think you'd never been to a cotillion before."

Stopped for the moment, Eleanor allowed herself to be led past city hall to a corner building and up the stairs to the Masons' lodge on the third floor.

The ballroom looked like fairyland. It was lit with an extravagant number of candles, and dancers and orchestra glowed in the soft light, the gowns of the women set off by the slender figures of the men. Facing each other in a formal line, one pair after another joined hands to take their turns dancing down the row to the instructions called from the orchestra in the corner.

Small as the room was, only a dozen or so could dance at a time, and the walls were ringed with chairs for matrons and wallflowers, who watched the dancers and exchanged gossip and news about current family affairs. Eleanor would have preferred going in during a pause in the music, when everyone's attention wasn't on the dancers, but her mother pushed her inside when nobody was looking except some elderly matrons, who raised their fans and whispered in each other's ears the minute she appeared.

Eleanor firmly in tow, Penelope Passmore Carpenter made her way down the row to some empty chairs, nodding along the way to acquaintances, who one by one cut off their talk and snapped their fans shut as she and Eleanor walked by. Sam went off to join the men at the end of the room, and Mrs. Carpenter sat down beside a young matron, who returned her greeting with the deference appropriate to a Passmore—and instantly put the Squire's lady into an agreeable frame of mind. Mrs. Carpenter pointedly complimented the young woman on her grey dress, though her remark didn't hit its target.

Eleanor couldn't see anything but the dancers. Disappointed there, she studied the men Sam was talking with. McMaster, however, wasn't to be seen, and Eleanor had to sit like a stranded mermaid, answering her neighbor's occasional questions with attention totally elsewhere. By now her mother was happily aswim in her own element, while Eleanor sat morosely and wished she hadn't come to the cotillion. Her gloom continued through two more dances, till her brother broke from the men he'd been talking with about Jackson's progress to Washington. Finally Sam led her onto the floor, giving Mrs. Carpenter the pleasure of showing off the deportment of her Passmore children.

Her partner was only her brother and not the one she wanted, but Eleanor's spirits rose as soon as she was dancing. Hand held high in Sam's, she couldn't resist showing off just a bit. By the third figure she'd forgotten everything but the pleasure of the moment. The dance ended too soon, and her spirits plummeted when Sam escorted her back to her chair.

Only, however, till the crowd of dancers thinned, and she saw a dark figure talking to Penelope Carpenter with the politeness due from a recent house guest. Fast as her heart beat, Eleanor acknowledged Nicholas McMaster's stiff bow with a remark that struck even her as trite and, for the first time in her life, made her feel awkward. Sam, on the other hand, greeted McMaster warmly and, to Eleanor's chagrin, drew him away to talk about political twistings in Washington and Harrisburg.

Supper was a special trial, when the men went into another room to be served at table, while Eleanor was left with the women to balance a plate on her knees and enjoy the pleasure of female company. She had to endure the attentions of her mother's friends and their uncomfortable questions about her husband's health — Mrs. Carpenter having insisted on keeping up the fiction of an extended family visit. Some of the women asked pointedly after Alec's friend Gilbert as well, bringing red spots to Eleanor's cheeks and her mother's foot heavily stamped on hers.

Eleanor sighed with relief when the dining room doors finally opened, and men began to trickle back in, a signal for the orchestra to reassemble and again strike into music. Sam and McMaster were among the last to come back, still deep in conversation. But they made their way to Mrs. Carpenter and Eleanor, and in a moment were leading mother and daughter onto the floor to join the dance.

Eleanor's spirits soared again, though the complicated figures hardly gave a chance for more than flying questions and remarks. Still, Eleanor finally made the one she'd been waiting for. "I have to talk with you, Nick," she said, when their hands joined momentarily.

Whatever McMaster thought, his expression didn't change. A few minutes later, as he led her through another figure, he said softly, "Excuse yourself to take some air, and I'll find a way to join you."

When the dance was over and Eleanor again seated beside her mother, she fanned herself ostentatiously and complained about the heat. Tired by her own recent exertions, Penelope Carpenter furled and spread her fan in exasperation, then ordered Eleanor to take a turn in the air as an alternative to sharing her complaints, hardly surprised that her butterfly of a daughter couldn't stay in one room for the duration of an evening.

Pretending boredom, Eleanor left the ballroom, fetched her cloak, and made her way to the front door. Once outside, she rested on the step and inhaled the crisp air, momentarily enjoying the cold after the stuffiness inside. She'd just begun to shiver when McMaster joined her.

Instead of greeting her affectionately, he said, "This is hardly a place to talk. Come," and led her across the square to the White Swan Hotel and a private sitting room.

As soon as they were alone, Eleanor expected an embrace. She'd half decided to resist (at least at first). Instead, to her surprise, McMaster stood stiffly, watching her with his head tilted. "Aren't you glad to see me, Nick?" she asked, puzzled.

"Of course, my dear," he replied. "I'm always delighted to see someone as charming as you."

Taken aback, Eleanor stared at him with astonishment she didn't try to hide as, hands clasped behind his back, McMaster continued, "Still, it is awkward to be called from a public function for a private interview."

Her eyes growing wider with every one of his words, Eleanor could only blurt, "But you said we'd see each other at the cotillion. Except for that, I wouldn't have come — and had to spend hours with those tedious women!"

"I thought you'd enjoy the ball," McMaster answered, smiling faintly. "I'm sorry you mistook my meaning — or thought I had anything else in mind."

Flustered, Eleanor fluttered her fan nervously, then shut it with a snap. "What did you expect me to think?" she asked.

"How can I presume on the thoughts of a beautiful woman?" McMaster answered, with the same infuriating smile. "I was glad to see you, of course, and know that you were enjoying society again."

"Is that the only reason you were glad to see me?" Eleanor retorted, the shock of surprise rapidly giving way to anger. "You know very well that I only came because you told me you'd be here."

"And so I am," McMaster replied, cutting her off before she could say any more. "That's precisely what I told you, and I've been as good as my word." Seeing the working of her face, he stepped forward and seized her arms. "Look at me," he ordered, as she turned away. "I want you to look me in the eye and tell me if I ever said I'd do more than see you here." When she didn't answer, he shook her. "Answer me, Eleanor," he demanded.

In spite of herself, Eleanor glanced at him and slowly raised her head to meet the full force of his look. "Did I tell you anything except that we'd see each other here?" he insisted. Dumbly, she shook her head. "Now listen," he went on in the same even voice. "We enjoyed each other's company over Christmas, and that's as much as a married woman can expect." He paused to be sure she was absorbing his words.

As though she were in the middle of a dream, Eleanor stared at him. "I'm not married now," she managed to whisper.

Satisfied that she was past danger of an outburst, McMaster released her arms. "No," he said, stepping back and repeating her words, "you're not married now. Now, my dear Eleanor, you're divorced, and that makes you more of a problem."

"I—I don't understand," Eleanor stuttered, dumbfounded. "Because of you, I'm free—I thought you wanted me free." She stopped without explaining the reasons her imagination had supplied.

But McMaster answered like a mind reader. "In a manner of speaking you're free," he said. "The divorce makes you free from Johns, but it doesn't make you the single lady you were before you married him. In brief, Miss Eleanor, in the eyes of the law you're free from your husband and free to marry again. But in the eyes of society, your situation is—shall I say—difficult? In fact, your evening with the ladies might have been worse if they'd known your position. After all," McMaster concluded, "society doesn't open its collective arms to a divorced woman."

Eleanor could feel the blood pounding in her temples. "The new president," she said faintly. "He married a divorced woman."

With the same smile, McMaster answered, "And you know the trouble it caused him. I'll tell you plainly, once and for all. No politician short of a war hero can afford to compromise himself with a woman of less than impeccable reputation."

If he said more, Eleanor didn't hear. Her next conscious moment, she was sitting in a chair, while a strange woman held salts against her nose. Eleanor sneezed and heard a hateful voice saying, "She didn't feel well, and I brought her here. Look after her while I find her mother."

A few minutes later Sam and Mrs. Carpenter found the flower of the Passmores, sadly wilted, in a sitting room of the White Swan. Acidly, the Squire's lady remarked to her son that life in Christiana had apparently unsettled his sister for the rigors of proper society.

12.

Early March saw drinks aplenty downstairs at the Fox. Three
months after being chosen by the state electors, Andrew
Jackson had been officially inaugurated, and John Skiles, for
one, toasted the new president and made no bones of declaring
to all and sundry that the Union was finally on the high road to
democracy.

"What did I tell you?" Skiles exclaimed from his seat by the
fire, waving his flip glass under the nose of Tall Hen, who sat
morosely at the far end of the settee sipping a mug of cider.
"Fifty years of presidents, and which other one you ever seen
that opened up the White House and let in ordinary folks, yet? I
tell you, things is gonna be different from here on in," Skiles
pronounced.

Possibly because he'd escaped to the Fox from a fight with
his wife, possibly because his seat was in line with the draft
from the door, Tall Hen wasn't convinced. "Maybe so, maybe
not," he answered. He took a pull from his mug and wiped his
mouth against his sleeve. "From what I hear tell," he said, "it's

gonna cost a pretty penny to put the place back together again after that party. And he ain't done so hot yet by the Amalgamation you were so het on, either. You said Jackson was the man for the people, but all he's done so far is favor them bigwigs down in Philadelphia. We might as well have Adams yet, for all I can see."

Snorting contemptuously, Skiles sat back. "Henry Diffenderfer, if you can't see no difference between them that's for us and them that's against us, I give up on you. Who ever learned you about politics, anyhow?"

The argument might have lasted all morning if Tall Hen hadn't sneezed. "Drat the door," he muttered, pulling a crumpled handkerchief from his pocket and blowing his nose.

Meanwhile, Skiles was studying the doorway. "Shut the door!" he shouted, "if you wasn't born in a barn!"

The man closed it hesitantly and stepped inside. He was very small and, even in his bulky homespun coat, strangely birdlike, as he swiveled his head to dart glances from one corner of the room to another, while his eyes adjusted to the light.

"Come on over to the fire and warm yourself onct," Skiles called, half inviting and half ordering. His nosiness overweighing his sense of proprietorship, he moved from the center of the settee and made room for the stranger next to the fire, while Tall Hen eyed his friend resentfully and again exploded into his handkerchief.

"Where you come from?" Skiles asked, barely giving the little man time to loosen his coat. Hands stretched to the fire, the stranger continued studying the room, moving his head in jerky motions, as though his eyes were fixed and only turning his neck let him see what wasn't in front of his nose. As his neck swiveled, his eyes stopped on Skiles. "I come all the way from home," he said.

"If I hadn't knowed that already, I wouldn't of asked," Skiles retorted, aiming a squirt of tobacco juice at the fire and missing.

"If you knowed already, then you shouldn't of asked," Tall Hen commented spitefully.

Skiles ignored him and took another tack. "You from around here?" he asked the stranger.

This question was a bit more successful. "No, only my brother used to be," the man answered, still swiveling his head and studying the room. Skiles nodded sagely to Tall Hen, before he turned back to the stranger and asked his name. "Bertie Wilson," the man answered. Thawed by the fire, he added that he'd been told to ask for Will Carpenter, Esquire, who was executing his brother's will. "Miles died a couple months back," he added, "but he lived around here before that."

"Sharp as the Squire is, maybe he's guillotining that will too," Skiles declared, slapping his knee, then seeing the blank looks of his listeners, going on to explain. "You maybe know what that is — it's taking a sharp knife and cutting things up into little pieces and keepin' the head in a basket for hisself. That's French, in case you didn't know. And the Squire's sharp enough for it," he added, again slapping his knee.

Tall Hen glared at him, while Bertie Wilson smiled politely. Nevertheless, Skiles was helpful enough to the visitor, indicating that the tapster at the grate was only the German redemptioner. A free mug of flip in hand, he even huffed himself off the settee and into the kitchen to send Catherine upstairs with word of the Squire's visitor, while, his own glass empty, Tall Hen glared after him more resentfully than ever.

Busy over dinner, Catherine didn't waste time before she sent the little man up to the Squire's office, though he halted confusedly on his way through the kitchen and aimed a quick bow at Eleanor, who was sitting at the table, before he darted up the steps.

To Catherine, it seemed that lately Eleanor had turned into a fixture in the kitchen. Nights, the piano sounded only in brief spurts, generally breaking off discordantly after a few bars. Moreover, the daughter of the Fox and flower of the Passmores had changed. If anything, she was dressed more carefully than ever, but her silence disconcerted Catherine, after the string of babble she'd gotten used to.

After all the fuss Eleanor had made about the Birthday Ball, Catherine was disappointed not to get a description of it, just when Eleanor had made her curious about an event so strange. But instead of elaborate descriptions of ballroom and dresses, Catherine's questions brought only the tersest of replies and, finally, an exclamation that Eleanor had never suffered through a duller evening. Catherine stared in surprise but held her tongue. The excited chatter about Nicholas McMaster, too, had stopped as abruptly as Eleanor's dreams of the ball, Catherine discovered, when she asked if Eleanor had seen him.

"Don't mention that man," Eleanor snapped, her face drawn and resentful. "I don't want to think about him."

Catherine drew her own conclusions, which didn't cast credit on McMaster or Eleanor Johns. A farm girl like Catherine knew the facts of life, and Martha's threat to Eleanor in the spring house hadn't been lost on her. Clearly, more had passed between Eleanor and Nicholas McMaster than the rest of the household knew. And just as clearly, since the Birthday Ball, McMaster had changed from Eleanor's Prince Charming to something different.

In spite of her moral judgments, Catherine was sorry that Eleanor's hopes had been dashed, though her original aversion to McMaster was only stronger now. Eleanor, however, was too childlike to bear more blame than a butterfly who'd laid its eggs in a cabbage patch. Catherine almost pitied her, as Eleanor sat staring silently into the fire, while Catherine bustled about the kitchen.

With an hour till dinner had to be laid upstairs, Catherine wasn't especially busy yet. Cheeks pink from working by the fire and eyes sparkling, she dropped cheerful remarks to Eleanor, trying to draw her out of her gloom. But the tidbits of information she passed on about doings in the countryside hadn't any more effect than her questions about Eleanor's music, evoking only, "I envy you, Catherine."

Catherine looked up from the haunch of venison she was

basting. "Seems to me I should envy you," she said, "with your pretty dresses and rich pap. I'll change places with you anytime you want," she said teasingly, " — and you can cook dinner and lay the table."

"I wish we could trade places and I could be you," Eleanor went on, staring at her lap and nervously pleating folds into her skirt.

Catherine laughed. "Seems to me, you'd have to be born all over again for that," she said, imagining Eleanor Johns at the farm and trying to picture her kneeling at morning prayers. "Maybe you could get by in the new place," she added. Suddenly remembering her father's troubles, she stopped, then, seeing Eleanor's misery, briskly added that even there, she'd have to hustle to get by in the Landis family. "You'd have to hitch up your petticoats for the barn work," Catherine concluded, "and Mama would keep you busy in the house."

Eleanor looked up, temporarily distracted by the unusual picture. "What would I have to do?" she asked.

"Why, bake and clean and make butter and tend chickens and look after the garden, anyhow," Catherine answered, adding after a moment, "and then there's the baby yet."

Eleanor gave a start and stared at Catherine with frightened eyes. "The baby?" she asked softly.

Pleased to see Eleanor come out of her recent silence, Catherine smiled and gave another stir to the kettle she was inspecting. "My tongue got away. I forgot. I'm not supposed to tell, but pretty soon I'll have a new brother or sister."

A rush of color came over Eleanor's face. "Oh," she said quietly. "I didn't know."

Since she'd let the news slip, Catherine shrugged and explained that the new Landis was expected in two months. "When it comes, I'll have to go home and keep house," she added. "Mama's been sick, and she's worried this time." Noticing Eleanor's intent look, she was touched at her concern.

"But you can't leave!" Eleanor exclaimed. "What will I do without you? Papa won't let you!"

"You'll get on without me same as you did before I got here," Catherine answered slowly. "Your mam knows about it." After a moment she added, "She asked me to come back when Mama's well again."

"And you're going to," Eleanor retorted. "Promise you'll come back as soon as you can."

Instead of answering, Catherine bent to ladle some apple butter out of a crock. When she straightened up, she started to describe the news about the progress of Patience Slack, now living in Lancaster and, word had it, no better than she should be, to judge from the improved state of her wardrobe and the number of male visitors to her dirty, rented rooms. "From what I hear, she's quite the lady now," Catherine ended, shaking her head.

To her surprise, Eleanor flared back angrily, "I don't see why it's anybody's business what she does. She has to get by, and if she hasn't got anybody to help her, she has to do what she can, right or wrong!"

Catherine again shook her head. "You don't know her," she said. "That one only does what's easiest. After all, everybody's got choices, and we're held to account if we make the wrong ones."

Abruptly, Eleanor rose from her chair, knocking over the dish of apple butter and spilling it over the table. "I don't visit with you to hear Mennonite sermons," she said angrily. "Next thing you'll be preaching to me about turning the other cheek and never going to law and all the other twaddle you people talk!"

Catherine looked at her in surprise. "Saying the truth isn't making a sermon," she said simply, then shrugged and set about wiping up the spill, as Eleanor flounced up the stairs.

Almost immediately, Catherine heard a clatter and a shriek, then a small, apologetic voice saying, "I do beg your pardon, Miss." She hurried to the stairwell in time to see a flash of Eleanor's petticoat and Bertie Wilson picking himself up from the step where he was sitting, dazed.

"She bowled me right over," he said, shaking his head, as Catherine helped him down the stairs and into the chair Eleanor had left. His arm felt so fragile that she hoped the little man hadn't broken any bones, at the same time trying not to laugh at the look on his face.

"You'll be all right once you catch your breath," she said, and hurried into the taproom to fetch a mug of cider for him and compose her expression.

Bertie Wilson took the mug gratefully and raised it to his mouth, taking short, birdlike sips. "Oh dear!" he chirped after the third one, "this has been an upsetting trip!"

Hardly managing to keep a straight face, Catherine tried to console him. "Mrs. Johns didn't see you on the stairs, or she'd of been more careful," she offered.

The little man frowned. "Getting knocked up the steps wasn't the half of it," he said indignantly. "If that's the daughter of the house, running me over is the least I could of expected, after talking with her pap. The gall of that man!" he added.

Ruffled as he was, Wilson was obviously ready to share his indignation, and Catherine was curious enough not to stop him. When John Skiles sent her upstairs with word of the visitor, he'd mentioned that the little man was one of the Wilson heirs, and her father's plans had been too upset by Miles Wilson's death for her not to be interested. All that she had to do was look at him inquiringly, and Wilson's brother began to sing out his grievances like a ruffled sparrow.

"My own brother!" he exclaimed, exploding phrases in staccato bursts. "The money belongs to the family! We're all poor! But that Squire says we can't touch it! It's tied up. Legal thing, red tape—and all because that wild man Orson went to be a trapper and is off someplace in Kentucky!" His face red with anger, Bertie Wilson picked up the cider, threw back his head, and, in one swallow, tossed down what was left.

Taken aback by his outburst, Catherine shook her head. "A body can't do much against the law," she said consolingly.

"The law my foot!" Wilson shot back. "You can't tell me this ain't Carpenter's twistings and twinings. He's got his hands on my money, and he's turning the law any way he wants so's he can hang onto it. But it ain't justice, and it ain't right, and I won't let him get away with it!"

He pushed back his chair and stood up, looking taller than he had earlier (though he was still a head shorter than Catherine). "Thank you, Miss," he said politely. "I'll be going now, since I got to travel some."

Knowing only that he came from someplace in the South, Catherine asked, "Is your place far?"

"It's a good piece," Wilson answered, "but not as far as Kentucky. And I'll get what's coming to me, if I have to comb every square inch of that godforsaken place." Thanking her again for her kindness, he marched out of the Fox, leaving Catherine to ponder over his visit while she finished getting everything ready for the Squire's dinner.

13.

*F*rom Catherine's visits to the farm, it was clear that she'd be leaving the Fox before much longer. Her mother's full apron was now fastened high under her arms, and her face was tired and drawn. When Catherine was outside with her, Elizabeth turned her head to avoid seeing the new house. "It brings to mind a skull," she said and began to cough.

At least the days were getting longer as the equinox approached. Fields were brown from fresh ploughing, and trees were beginning to show a faint haze of green. The change in seasons, however, signalled more work as spring washing approached, when Mrs. Carpenter hired extra help to scrub dirty linen, and soap had to be made from lard and fat accumulated through the winter.

As sometimes happened when there was something extra to do, Mrs. Belcher had another asthma attack, leaving Catherine to do it. A fire was set near the oven, and Catherine and Davy were busy carrying out pans and crocks of grease, when, bells jingling, a familiar wagon lumbered down the lane and into the courtyard. Walking beside his horses, the wagoner pulled his team up by the carriage shed, as, his chore of the moment finished, Davy disappeared into the stable. As if he had nothing better to do, the lanky redhead ambled over to survey Catherine's preparations. "Is that all you got done, when it's going on noon?" he asked.

Catherine snapped up from the crock she was scraping, but instead of firing back angrily, she caught the wagoner's grin.

"Ach, Jake Good," she said, "you'll say anything to make me mad."

"You're pretty when your dander's up," he said, "and how else can I get you to pay attention to me?"

Catherine flushed and bent back to her work. She hadn't forgotten Christmas and the pretty, dark-haired girl Jake took home. "Seems to me," she said, "one girl at a time should give you attention enough, yet."

Jake was startled. "I ain't got a girl," he said. "What gave you that notion?"

"Maybe not," Catherine answered pertly, "only it looked like it at Christmas."

His face clearing, Jake whistled. "It looks to me like you're jealous," he retorted.

"No I ain't," Catherine shot back.

"Then I sure wish you was," he said. "The girl I wanted wasn't going no place and my cousin got left flat when her brother found a girl to take home." He grinned and added, "Still jealous?"

"I never was," Catherine insisted, but couldn't help asking, "Was she really your cousin?"

"Of course not," Jake said. "She's just another of the ones I make up to. Sailors, they don't hold a candle to wagoners, and I got one lined up every five miles."

"Maybe that's why it took you a month to get back here," Catherine said, scooping more lard into the pot, but sure that Jake didn't have any other girls down the road. Glancing around, she asked abruptly, "Did Jim's brother get away all right?"

Jake picked up another crock for her. "We can talk easier if people think I'm making up while I'm helping you," he said.

Catherine bent over to hide her smile and warned him that she didn't want any nonsense, and Jake smiled back. "I'm as sober as if I got the Bible with the lot in it," he said. Dropping his voice, he explained how he got Cassius away from the Fox, working him out of the oven legs first.

Noticing that Catherine had stopped scooping to listen, Jake interrupted himself. "You'd better shussle some or old lady Carpenter will be out here and shoo me off," he warned.

"Anyhow," he said, resuming his story, "I saw a candle upstairs, so there wasn't much time till the Squire'd be out — a good half hour earlier than anyone else —, so I scooted Cassius to the wagon and hightailed it out of here the minute I got the team hitched. We must of been halfway to Enterprise before Davy got started firing up the oven. But I couldn't risk keeping him," he went on, "when I might get searched, so near the crick just this side of Enterprise I pulled up, set him out, and pointed him towards Dan Gibbons' place."

When Catherine looked up in surprise, Jake explained that Gibbons looked after runaways and sent them off towards Canada. "Those Quakers are like that," he added meditatively, "but not many of us Mennonites ever reach out past the people at church."

"I didn't know anyone around here was mixed up in helping slaves," Catherine said quietly and asked if Cassius was likely to make it to Canada.

"Can't tell," Jake answered. "At least now he's got a chance to be free, only it wonders me sometimes if anyone ever is. Here you are, say, working for the Squire, and here I am, working to buy a farm, and it seems to me like neither of us got much chance to cut loose and do what we want, till we get the obligations we got taken care of. Like right now," he added, cocking his chin in the direction of the house.

Catherine looked over and saw Penelope Carpenter making

towards them in full sail, ready to overlook the soapmaking and insure that no young woman working for her was wasting time with any young man—at least on time she was paying for.

"I wanted to tell you, Katlie. I won't be bringing the team this way much more for now," Jake said hurriedly. "Pap needs me home for spring planting." When Catherine's disappointment showed on her face, he added, "But I'll get down to see you one way or another."

The mistress of the Fox ignored Jake's respectful greeting and pointedly inquired whether Catherine was done with the preparations. "Jake was just helping me finish up," Catherine answered, whereupon Mrs. Carpenter looked at the young man icily and remarked that Catherine had work to do.

Jake shrugged and ambled back to his team, which was soon jingling out the lane and down the road towards Columbia, while, turning to Catherine, Mrs. Carpenter wasted no time in telling her that she was being paid to work, not flirt with young men—"especially," she added, "when he didn't even stop in the taproom. I won't have loose behavior in my household, and I expect you to remember that."

Catherine clenched her teeth to keep back an angry retort, thinking to herself that Mrs. Carpenter had one set of rules for help and another for family. Still, in short order she was busy enough with the soapmaking to put aside her indignation.

For the next hour or two Mrs. Carpenter was in and out of the inn, checking that Catherine used enough lye to set the soap and enough lime to whiten it. After two batches came out all right, Catherine was finally left to enjoy working on her own.

As the morning wore on, the sun cut through the earlier haze, while the usual bustle of visitors came and went in the sunshine, including John Skiles, who made a point of waddling over to Catherine and stood squinting alternately at her and the kettle. "My mam never stirred it with no sassafras stick," he commented critically, "but I guess you people got your own way of doing stuff."

Catherine nodded and went on with her work, and, his

nosiness satisfied, Skiles disappeared into the taproom to take his usual place and wait for gossip. Some boys from up the road came by to loiter beside the lean-to where the eagle huddled, and slightly later Eleanor Johns came down the outside steps and made her way across the courtyard.

Catherine called and waved to her, but to her surprise, Eleanor walked on without turning her head. Opposite the eagle she hesitated, but the boys were still standing there with their hands stuffed in their pockets, and Eleanor continued past the sheds to a path that led up a grade behind the Fox.

Catherine watched her out of sight, then shrugged and went on with her work. The dressing down she'd gotten from Mrs. Carpenter rankled as she sweated over the fire, and she was disappointed at Eleanor's fickleness. Catherine told herself she'd known better than to trust a fine lady, but she was lonesome at the Fox and had grown fond of Eleanor in spite of herself. Still, it was clear to her that friendship meant more to some people than it did to others.

In another half hour she'd poured the last batch of soap and looked around for Davy, but, as usual, he'd slipped away when she needed him. Catching sight of Jim, she called him, and, good-naturedly, he helped her carry the kettle to the pump so she could start washing up.

Gumbo had just turned back towards the stable, when he stopped. "You hear that, Missy?" he asked. They both listened, as high-pitched calls came closer, and Davy came running down the path, past the boys still loitering near the eagle and across the courtyard, shouting in gasps with the wind he had to spare. He shot towards the taproom door, but at a hail from Gumbo veered towards the pump, his eyes round and freckles standing out starkly on his frightened face.

He was so winded that he could hardly talk between pants, just gasp, "Mrs. Johns!"

Gumbo shook Davy's shoulders. "Calm down, boy!" he said, "or you'll never get out what you got to say."

"Mrs. Johns!" the boy gasped again "—in the field!" He

wiggled around and flung an arm towards where he'd come.

"Easy, boy, easy," Gumbo said, as if he was calming a nervous horse, while, thoroughly frightened, Catherine felt her scalp tingle. "Miss Eleanor's in the field. Now, what else you got to tell?"

Davy's eyes got even rounder. "She's layin' in the dirt," Davy said. "And she's all bloody!"

For a long moment man and boy stared at each other, while, incongruously, Catherine thought of the pictures in the *Martyrs Mirror*. A fraction of a second later, Gumbo released the boy, who wheeled around and ran back the way he'd come, Gumbo loping at his heels and calling to Catherine to rouse the Squire.

Catherine rushed to the kitchen, where Martha Carpenter was doing duty in her place. "Something's happened to Eleanor!" she exclaimed. "Where's your pap?"

Martha paused midway in pouring meal into a pot of water. "Stir this," she said, dumping in the rest and thrusting the spoon at Catherine before she disappeared up the kitchen steps. In a minute or so, heavy feet pounded down the stairs, and the Squire burst into the room.

"What the blazes is going on?" he thundered, so roughly that Catherine cringed. She stuttered out what she'd heard from Davy, while the Squire glared at her as if whatever had happened was her fault, all the more angry because she didn't know more. He hurried outside, going as fast as a man of his bulk and dignity could without breaking into a run.

Catherine gave an impatient stir to the kettle and took it off the fire, then went to the door, where the courtyard suddenly bustled with activity. One of the neighbor boys was shouting and gesturing up the path, and John Skiles was standing at the matching door, morosely watching some cronies disappear up the path, since even such a choice opportunity for news was currently impossible for a man of his girth. Still, he was blaring out his opinions to an equally inactive neighbor.

"It chust goes to show how the country's goin' to the dogs," Skiles proclaimed, "when a woman can't even take a walk on her own pap's own land, without she's attacked by some tramp."

"Ach, Chon," said his companion, "you was sayin' chust a couple months back, we was on the high road to heaven, now Jackson's runnin' things."

"Maybe I did," Skiles answered, pulling in his horns a bit, "only I didn't know no more than you did then how he'd run things. Still, I can't fault him, seein' that the country's gone this bad, so's even Jackson can't make it over in a month. And I tell you, this here's just one more sign of what ailed the democracy till he got voted in." Gathering steam as he went, Skiles demanded, "When's the last time you heard tell on a woman gettin' murdered on her own pap's back stoop?"

John Skiles never made pronouncements quietly, and Catherine staggered against the door frame, only to be knocked from behind by the mistress of the Fox, who pushed past her, wringing her hands and looking around distractedly. Catherine slipped to one side to make room for Martha, following at her mother's heels and trying to calm her.

"Where is she?" Mrs. Carpenter exclaimed to anyone in earshot, her usual calm broken but more imperious than ever. His neighbor looked at Skiles, waiting for him to answer, but Skiles was used to pontificating among equals and too tongue-tied to answer the Squire's lady.

"Are all of you deaf and dumb?" Penelope Carpenter exploded, looking around angrily. "I want to know where my daughter is!"

"Davy says she's up there somewhere," Catherine said, pointing towards the path. Without a glance at her cook, Mrs. Carpenter launched herself across the courtyard. She was halfway when Gumbo came loping down the grade. He paused to exchange a few words with his mistress before she disappeared up the path, while Gumbo ran to the stable. Martha and Catherine followed in time to see him grabbing up horse blankets. He was ready to rush out again, when Martha blocked his way.

"What's happened up there?" she demanded, looking every bit as square and forceful as the Squire. "Is Eleanor dead?"

Gumbo paused and dipped his head in a quick gesture of respect. "She ain't quite dead," he answered, "but she sure ain't got much life left, and she's cut real bad." He emphasized the last two words. Realizing that Martha wasn't going to move without more information, he added, "Squire's bound her up best way he can and wants blankets so we can get her back to the house."

She flinched at his words, but Martha Carpenter wasn't ready to let him go yet, while, knowing better than to cross even the least of the Carpenters, Gumbo gripped the blankets nervously, ready to bolt the moment he had the chance.

"Do they know who did it?" Martha demanded.

"Got some idea," Gumbo answered reluctantly, fixing his eyes on some harness near the door. "The Squire, he found a razor right next to her," Gumbo continued after a pause. Finally, he glanced at Martha. "Squire cursed some when he saw it there layin' in the dirt, but first thing he said when he clapped his eyes on it was, 'Why, that's my very own razor.'" Refusing to look at Martha again, he added, "It looks like she done it to herself."

Martha stepped aside. "Take the blankets," she said. Gumbo bobbed his head and bolted from the stable, while Catherine and Martha stood motionless, stunned to hear that Eleanor Johns had apparently tried to take her own life.

14.

$\mathcal{T}$he Fox stayed in a bustle for the next week, as people from the neighborhood stopped by the taproom, hoping to pick up news on what had happened to Eleanor Johns. Catherine had been called home, and the most visitors could learn from a wheezing Mrs. Belcher was that, in his capacity as justice of the peace, the Squire had issued a warrant for the arrest of a person or persons unknown, charged with attacking his daughter, Eleanor Carpenter Johns.

As a result, fear curdled the peace of the countryside. Wives on isolated plantations harried their husbands to put bolts on the doors, and equally worried husbands found new and more ingenious places to hide their savings. Suddenly, any stranger was eyed with suspicion, while stories passed from family to family about pilfered smokehouses and missing poultry. Everyone in the township was in a state of alarm — everyone, that is, except Gumbo Jim, who shook his head over the rumors but held his tongue.

Naturally, questions focused on the condition of Eleanor

Johns, who lay in her room, weak from loss of blood, and, rumor had it, numbed and broken and showing no interest in returning where a lady could be treated so badly. Sophia Passmore, her favorite aunt, had been sent for. In the meantime, everything possible was being done for the sufferer, though the doctor from Lancaster shook his head and declared that it was touch and go whether or not she'd survive the shock, knowing that his credit was safe either way.

What had really happened, of course, had to be told to her brother, when he got back from a trip to Philadelphia, and to her Aunt Sophie, who arrived with her travelling bag three days after Eleanor's accident.

Sophia Passmore was the elder of Major Passmore's two daughters and the beauty of the family. Although she'd had her share of beaux, she never married, seeing no reason to give up her independence, when she inherited enough money to live on her own and do what she liked. She had a house in Columbia but seldom stayed in it, spending most of her time travelling about and looking after family crises. Most of the relatives had rooms waiting for her.

In an unassertive way, Sophia Passmore was as firm in her opinions as Martha and every bit as elegant as Eleanor. And her judgments were listened to, especially because she'd parlayed her inheritance into a comfortable income from canny investments, using business sense that even Will Carpenter respected.

She arrived at the Fox Monday night, after taking the coach to Lancaster and transferring to the one for the Old Road, having refused her brother-in-law's offer to meet her in the city because she preferred, on principle, to get where she wanted on her own.

Penelope Passmore Carpenter had been watching for her anxiously and lost no time in taking her to her room, where her sister insisted on composing herself after her hours of jolting and refused to hear any hint of the family troubles till she'd freshened up and had a bite to eat. Fragile and petite as she looked, she had a spine like an ivory knitting needle, and Penelope had to wait till Sophie was ready to consider the current family problem. Only after she'd finished some chicken and wiped her mouth and fingers delicately, did she let her sister explain what had happened, listening carefully as Penelope described Eleanor's attempt at suicide and the Squire's ploy for hiding the truth. "She never would have tried it except for her Carpenter blood," Penelope ended. "No Passmore ever did anything so disgraceful."

Her sister's pronouncement passed without comment from Sophie, who inquired into the recent state of Eleanor's spirits, sifting for information to explain her niece's action. The most she got from Penelope, however, was the description of a great uncle of her husband's who suffered from melancholia all his life, shut himself off from the family, and died a recluse.

Sophie listened while Penelope moved to Will Carpenter's even more distant relatives but interrupted when she started to describe a hypochondriacal cousin by marriage, breaking in to ask if Eleanor knew she'd arrived.

"It's hard to say," Penelope answered, checking herself and wiping her eyes. "We told her you were coming, but she wouldn't answer. Sophie, she won't even look at us, just turns her head and stares at the wall." Clearly, the Squire's lady was more upset than she'd been since they were girls, when a dearth of young men brought home to her that Will Carpenter was her only chance for a husband.

Judging that she'd gleaned as much as she was likely to for the moment, Sophie stood up and announced that she was ready to see her niece as soon as it was convenient, making clear that it was for her now. Obediently, Penelope led her down the corridor still lit by the far window and to the door of Eleanor's room, where Sophie turned and ordered her to get some rest. Penelope hesitated but turned back, while Sophie waited till her sister had started down the stairs, before she herself pressed the latch and entered Eleanor's room.

Between denunciations of the Carpenters' ancestry, Penelope had mentioned that Martha was with her sister because they were afraid to leave Eleanor alone, and Sophie saw Martha first, knitting in the failing light. Martha looked up with pleasure and relief, hurried over to her aunt, and held a whispered consultation with her. Then Martha lit a candle and slipped out the door, leaving her aunt to try her skill at calling up a response from the patient.

She took in the assorted bottles and glasses on the bedside table at a glance, then picked up the candle and held it over Eleanor's face. Instinctively, Eleanor flinched. Satisfied that she was awake, Sophie arranged her skirts and, straight and proper as if she were presiding at a tea party, sat down beside her.

"You can play possum with the others, Eleanor," she said crisply, "but it won't work with me, especially after I've jolted my bones into jelly to get to you. Besides," she added with a sigh, "heaven knows, you and I are enough alike that we know better than to play games with each other. I'm here, and I'm going to stay here till I get what I want." Leaning over the bed, she added, "And right now I want a greeting from my niece."

Instead of an answer, there was a sob from the bed. Sophie put her hand on Eleanor's shoulder. "It's all right, dear," she said resignedly. "I'm not in any hurry to get back in a coach, and bounce and rattle myself to Columbia just yet. I can wait." She patted Eleanor like a colicky baby and repeated, "I can wait."

But she didn't wait long till the bed started to shake with sobs. "It's all right, dear," Sophie said gently. "You'll feel better after a good cry."

Eleanor cried less and less controllably, while her aunt leaned over and rubbed her back. Finally, Sophie felt her niece relaxing. Calculating that the worst was past, she massaged Eleanor's shoulders till the girl was quiet, then briskly ordered her to sit up and blow her nose, simultaneously lifting her and arranging the bolster and pillow for a back rest.

Half resisting, Eleanor let herself be raised against the headboard, where her aunt propped her securely and immediately thrust a handkerchief at her with the order, "Now blow."

While Eleanor followed her aunt's instructions, Sophie studied her in the candlelight. The bandages on her wrists and throat gleamed eerily, but Sophie was more startled at Eleanor's pallor and the dark rims around her eyes, as though, after trying to kill herself, the girl already belonged as much with the dead as the living. But she only said, "A little more," and waited for Eleanor to give a few more weak puffs into the handkerchief, then leaned forward and wiped her nose.

"There," Sophie said. "That's more like it." In a few more minutes she was sitting on the bed and brushing Eleanor's tangled hair. "Now, don't turn away, young lady," she ordered. "I'm still waiting for a civilized greeting, and you know very well that I intend to get it. Are you ready to give me a kiss?"

Overpowered, Eleanor planted a weak kiss on her aunt's cheek, then hugged her convulsively. "I'm so glad to see you," she said, her voice so thin that a breeze through the shutters could have blown it away.

"At least you still have a tongue in your head," Sophie responded after planting an answering kiss on the invalid's cheek. She didn't show her relief — or wait to follow up her advantage.

"It's about time someone my age got a proper welcome," Sophie said, "and an explanation, too. As for that story your father gave out, I don't believe it for a minute, oh no. You'll have to come up with something better than that to satisfy your Aunt Sophie." Watching Eleanor sharply, she went on, "Why, any minute, they may pick up some poor wanderer, and before he can open his mouth, clap him in jail for an attack on the Squire's daughter."

Sophie accompanied her words with steady strokes of the brush, while she studied her niece. Eleanor winced and Sophie paused. "Did I hurt you, dear?" she asked primly. "I'm afraid I hit a rat's nest, if ever I saw one. I'll have to work it out with the comb. I'll try not to pull too hard, but it's bound to hurt.

"As I was just saying," Sophie continued, "I do hate to think what they'll do to any poor soul they pick up. Upset as people are, if he doesn't have the luck to fall in with Quakers or Mennonites, he may not make it as far as the jail." Caught in a tangle, the comb jerked Eleanor's head, and she squealed. "I am sorry, dear," Sophie remarked. "I told you it was bound to hurt, though I'll try not to pain you more than I have to.

"Blame has to fall somewhere," she resumed, "and whoever it falls on has to suffer. We can't avoid that." The comb again jerked Eleanor's head.

"There wasn't a tramp," Eleanor breathed, so softly that Sophie had to lean forward to catch what she said. "Maybe Papa told you that, but it's not true. I didn't mean to hurt anyone else."

Combing more evenly now, Sophie said, "Of course not, dear," and waited to hear more. "You went up to the field and deliberately cut yourself with your father's razor," Sophie finally spelled out, just as her comb hit another tangle. Eleanor gasped and whimpered, "Yes."

Again combing steadily, Sophie sighed, and, as if she were talking to herself, said, "The question is, why a young woman would deliberately try to do away with herself, especially one who didn't need money and was well rid of a bad husband. That's the real puzzle," she concluded, "because even a scatterbrain like you, Eleanor, wouldn't do something like that without a reason."

Eleanor didn't answer, and the comb hit a last convenient tangle. "What did you say, dear?" Sophia Passmore asked sweetly.

"Yes, Aunt Sophie," Eleanor said in a tiny voice.

"Now, I just wonder what kind of trouble could be so bad that a girl would rather die than face it," Sophie mused, combing steadily now. "But hard as I can think, there's only one kind that comes to me." She put down the comb, laid a hand on either side of Eleanor's face, and turned her into the light. Eleanor resisted feebly but was no match for the older woman.

Sophie peered into her face. Hesitantly, Eleanor raised her eyes to meet her aunt's sharp brown ones. "Eleanor," Sophia Passmore asked, "are you in the family way?"

"No!" Eleanor exclaimed and started to cry. Sophie let go of her, and Eleanor covered her face. "I didn't want anyone to know," she whispered. "And I didn't know what else to do."

Instead of commiserating with her niece, Sophia Passmore again presented Eleanor with the handkerchief. "I was afraid it had to be something like that," she answered simply. She didn't say more, and for several minutes the quiet was broken only by Eleanor's sobs. Then, from the lower reaches of the Fox, the Squire's clock chimed.

"It's not midnight yet," Sophie remarked, resuming her brusqueness, "and from the look of things, we have time to decide what to do. You get some rest now," she said, easing Eleanor back into bed and rearranging the bolster. "Now kiss me good night. We'll talk about it in the morning."

"Yes, Aunt Sophie," Eleanor answered.

It was several days till Sophie shared her information with the master and mistress of the Fox, having in the meantime squeezed as much information as she could from a reluctant Eleanor, who begged her aunt not to tell her parents that an extraneous member would join the Carpenter clan in September. "Like it or not, the family has to know," her aunt responded, "and the sooner the better. Trust me, dear." And Eleanor did because she had no choice.

Sophie passed word first to the shocked and disbelieving Penelope Passmore Carpenter, whose nostrils went white when she heard that Eleanor had been seduced by the guest she'd entertained at Christmas, all but taking him off the streets, as she put it, out of charity and the goodness of her heart. She seemed more upset at the slight to Passmore dignity than at Eleanor's predicament.

Squire Carpenter, however, took a different tack. His initial snorts of outrage and disbelief ended in a string of expletives directed at his daughter, whose indiscretion might end his association with as important a political ally as Nicholas McMaster.

Eleanor's sister Martha didn't react much to the news, as though she wasn't really surprised. Sam, on the other hand, was badly shaken and expressed his shock in a long whistle. "I didn't think Nick would go that far," he said, fingering his sideburns nervously, "or I'd never have asked him here."

In the next weeks the family legal expert rode to the Fox whenever he could spare a few hours, generally spending his visits in consultations with his aunt about what was to be done.

15.

For the last month Gideon Landis had been thinking of calling Catherine home. The new baby wasn't due till the end of April, and ordinarily Elizabeth could have carried on as usual. But things this time weren't ordinary. As her term wore on, Elizabeth got thinner and more drawn, as if the new life were draining the old one.

Added to his worry over Elizabeth was Gideon's bill to Owen Rees, the stone mason, who had extended the settlement date but, after waiting till March, was losing his patience. If that had been Gideon's only debt, he could have managed, but building the new house had involved other expenses as well, which Gideon was gradually paying off with the help of the children's earnings and Elizabeth's egg money. Rees was Gideon's biggest remaining creditor and obviously a disgruntled one, not likely to wait for his pay indefinitely.

He'd shown how disgruntled he was the week before, when he made a visit just as the family was sitting down to dinner. Sent to answer the door, Benny solemnly turned back to the table to give a stage whisper in German that the mason was there, a fact plain to the rest, because the Welshman was standing in the doorway. Refusing Elizabeth's invitation to eat, Rees instead called Gideon from the table and insisted on speaking with him outside, where, followed by Gideon, he stalked to the new house. "Would you say that's sound work?" he asked, slapping the stonework.

"No question on that," Gideon replied. "It's plenty sound."

"Are the stones matched and fitted proper?" Rees asked again, exploring the masonry with his fingers. "And how's the mortar holding up?" he continued. "Any problem with it washing out or crumbling in the rain? Did you see any cracks after that cold spell last winter?"

Wearily, Gideon shook his head. "It's as sound as I ever seen. I can't say one thing against the job you did."

"Never thought you could," the mason retorted. "I know my craft, and I give an honest day's work. Another thing," he continued briskly. "Would you say I charged too much for the work I did?"

Again, Gideon shook his head, trying to hide his shame and embarrassment and knowing full well the point of Rees's questions, which followed instantly.

The Welshman folded his arms and confronted Gideon like a banty rooster. "If you're telling me there's no problem with my work and the price was fair," he snapped, "then how come I ain't got paid yet?"

Unlike neighbors as practiced as John Skiles, Gideon had never before faced a creditor he couldn't pay. Too proud to give Rees excuses or grovel for sympathy, he could only ask for more time.

"More time!" exploded Rees. "Now, how much exactly did you have in mind? Were you thinking more like five days or five years? Landis," he continued, dropping his voice, "I want to know exactly when I'm getting my money."

Confronted with a direct demand, Gideon could only tell the truth. "I can't say," he replied, aware as he spoke that Rees wouldn't welcome his answer. "I'll get it to you as soon as I got it."

The mason met his statement with withering sarcasm. "You'll get it to me as soon as you got it," he repeated, mimicking Gideon's accent. "Well now, if you can't say, maybe I can, and I say I'm getting my money, and I'm getting it next week. You mark my words, Landis," he said, shaking his finger under Gideon's nose. "If I ain't paid by today a week, I'm handing my bill over to where I'll get paid for it all right, if I don't get nothing more than satisfaction." He pointed his chin towards the walls of the new house. "You wanted a new place to live, but if I don't get my money, you'll get one all right, right down on Prince Street where they put folks that don't pay their debts."

With a final shake of his finger, he stalked to his horse and scrambled onto it, deaf to Gideon's attempts to pacify him. Frustrated and fighting to keep down his own anger, Gideon watched him disappear before slowly returning to the kitchen.

Through the next week, Gideon made futile attempts to borrow what he needed to pay Rees. Naturally, he applied first to Squire Carpenter, in his capacity as semi-official banker for his corner of the township. The Squire, however, explained that currently he had nothing to spare, having just paid off a mortgage and used up his ready cash. Next, Gideon made a trip to Lancaster, where, starting with the Farmers', he applied unsuccessfully to each of the city's three banks. Not knowing what the next few days might bring, he stopped at the Fox on his way back and told Catherine to get ready to come home.

When Catherine told Mrs. Carpenter she was leaving shortly, the lady was as indignant as though she'd been personally insulted and cheated, though she'd been warned months before about Catherine's impending departure. "I counted on you at least through Easter," she said coldly, before adding some general remarks on the advantages of indentured servants, who always served out their terms. Catherine listened with as much patience as she could muster and packed her clothes.

She was leaving the Fox with her father before Catherine had her first inkling that Gideon might have called her home for a reason different than she thought. He'd brought the wagon, and as they bounced and jolted away from the inn, Catherine first vented her anger against Mrs. Carpenter and then asked how her mother was.

"She ain't good," Gideon answered, and added, "but she could be worse." He didn't say more till the wagon turned off the Old Road towards the farm.

Gideon seemed more laconic than usual, and his expression warned Catherine to wait for anything else he intended to tell her, while she hung onto her seat and studied the yellowish-green branches signalling the start of the new season. Gideon's eyes, however, stayed fixed on the road when he spoke next.

"Katlie," he said, "I want you to look after your mam and the boys." Having expected to do just that, Catherine answered only, "Sure, I'll do that, Pap."

Gideon shook his head. "You'll maybe have more to do than you know yet," he said, "if I get called away."

Catherine stared at him in surprise. "Why would you want to go away?" she asked.

Gideon didn't answer immediately. "It might not have to do with wanting to or not," he said finally. Then he added, "Now, don't ask no more questions—and don't say nothing to your mamma." Looking over at his daughter, his face softened. "I don't know yet that I'll have to," he said, "so we'll just leave it at that."

Catherine got a boisterous welcome from Benny and Paul and a quiet but heartfelt one from Elizabeth, who nevertheless sighed and remarked that she wished Peter were home and they could all be together.

"Now Mama," Gideon replied. "Peter's almost growed, and we can't keep them forever. Adam Wenger is giving him off tomorrow so he can have supper with us. He'll be home soon enough." But in spite of his soothing words, Gideon did his work mechanically, as if his mind were on something else.

The next day Elizabeth talked incessantly, barely letting Catherine out of sight except when, overcome with fatigue, she had to lie down. Meantime, Benny and Paul bounced in and out of the kitchen every chance they had, bringing unnecessary news of the farm animals or presenting their sister with feathers or dead weeds as homecoming gifts. They all looked forward to the afternoon, when Peter was coming home to join them for the evening meal.

Two hours before he was due, however, the Landises had less welcome visitors. Hearing the clop of horses and squawks from the poultry, Catherine looked out the window near the dry sink. The three men were strangers to her, and when she went outside to ask their business, she was surprised to see them leading an extra horse. Benny had been offering her another treasure, this one an arrowhead he'd found in the field Gideon was harrowing. When the strangers asked where her father was, Catherine sent the boy to guide them to where Gideon was working what was left of the field by the quarry.

Napping in the bedroom, Elizabeth woke and asked who Catherine had been talking to. "Just some men to see Pap," Catherine answered. "They said it's business," she added, urging her mother to get some sleep to be rested when Peter arrived.

Nevertheless, Elizabeth got up and came back to the kitchen as soon as she'd tidied her hair. "I shouldn't worry so," she explained, "but the way things have been going lately, I can't close my eyes for fear your pap may be getting more trouble." When Catherine tried to reassure her, she smiled wanly and shook her head. "When we got feelings about things, it don't help to talk them away," she said. She walked about restlessly, alternately going to the window and the door and not even bothering to check on Catherine's progress with the butter she was making, thanks to a cow that came in fresh earlier than expected.

She was peering out the door when the party of men reappeared, Gideon with them. Elizabeth watched as they stopped by the kitchen path. "What do they want, Mama?" Catherine asked from across the room.

"Hush up," her mother answered. "Your pap's talking to them, but I can't make out what they're saying. Now he's coming in, but those men ain't moved, like they're waiting on him."

Faster than was good for it, Catherine worked the butter, her attention, like her mother's, riveted on her father. She was just adding saffron when he got to the door, which Elizabeth pulled open, moving back to let him inside. Instead, he stopped on the threshold. "I can't come in," he said.

Elizabeth studied his face. "What do those men want, Gideon?" she asked. "It's more trouble, ain't?"

Gideon nodded. "It's no good holding back," he said finally. "Libby, I don't want you to fret and worry, but I got to go into Lancaster for a couple days."

Elizabeth's face was expressionless, as she asked in a low voice, "Why, Gideon? I'll worry more if I don't know."

Gideon shifted his eyes to the ground and didn't answer. One of the men in the lane called over, "Hurry on, Landis! We're waiting."

Gideon finally met his wife's eyes. "You might as well know sooner as later," he said. "Rees called for his money, and he's put the sheriff on me."

"Where are they taking you, Gideon?" Elizabeth asked in the same even voice.

"To jail," he said, in a voice as expressionless as hers. "I'll make what arrangements I can—God willing, it won't be long." The men called again from the lane, and Gideon bent down and kissed her, saying briefly, "The Lord keep you, Elizabeth." Abruptly, he turned, and, walking with quiet dignity, rejoined the waiting men, mounted the extra horse, and shortly was disappearing out the lane.

Catherine hadn't been able to hear the exchange between her parents. "Where's he going, Mama?" she asked, looking up from the butter she was scraping into the mold. Elizabeth was still standing at the open door, but as Catherine spoke, she stumbled against the door frame and grasped it for support. "I got to sit down," she said. Catherine wiped her hands and hurried to help her to a chair. Thoroughly frightened, she asked urgently, "What is it, Mama?"

Elizabeth sat with her eyes closed, her face like marble, except for the faintly moving lips. "Your father's been hauled to jail for debt," she said. Catherine flinched as if she'd been hit. Irrationally, her first thought was that that put an end to any courting from Jake Good. She raised her hand to her cheek as if she was feeling for a brand.

"He didn't tell me before," Elizabeth breathed, "only I knew it was coming." She closed her eyes while her lips continued to move silently, and Catherine knew she was praying.

Thuds from running feet signalled the return of the children, and Benny and Paul burst into the room, squabbling as they came. "He ain't either!" Benny insisted, his voice shrill.

"Is too!" Paul retorted. "What I said was right, ain't, Katlie?" Without waiting for an answer, he rushed on, "Those men took Pap off to jail, and that makes him a jailbird! — ain't so, Katlie? Benny says he ain't, but he is, and what I said is true!"

Before he could go on, Elizabeth's voice cut through the room. "Shame on both of you!" she pronounced in a voice brittle with anger. "I won't hear that kind of talk in this house. Don't you ever say a word against your pap again!"

Paul looked confused. He was used to correction but not the anger in his mother's voice. Before either child could say more, Catherine seized an arm of each and hurried them outside.

A green bench sat next to the door, and Catherine sank down on it, telling the boys that she wanted to talk to them and indicating places on either side. She was too numb to think of comforting them, but both burrowed against her, and, automatically, she put her arms around them.

"I don't see why Mama got mad when what I said was true," Paul grumbled, " 'cause if they took Pap to jail, then he's a jailbird."

"Is not," Benny said stubbornly. Both looked at Catherine.

"Is Pap a jailbird, Katlie?" Paul asked wistfully.

Trying to gather her wits, Catherine said slowly, "Remember what Mama said." Improvising, she went on after a moment, "A jailbird belongs in jail, but Pap don't belong there."

"See, I told you!" Benny said, ducking his head around Catherine to triumph over his brother.

"Then why'd they take him there?" demanded Paul, not satisfied by his sister's answer.

"Because he owes money he can't pay," Catherine answered, "and when people got debts, they have to go to jail till they're paid."

Paul gave an uncomfortable wiggle, obviously not satisfied. "Ach, don't rutch so," Catherine said irritably, but Paul wasn't finished cross-examining her. Pushing her arm away, he followed out his train of logic.

"If people have to go to jail when they can't pay their debts, then they belong there and Pap *is* a jailbird, no matter what you and Mama say!" Nevertheless, his lip quivered, and tears rolled onto his cheeks, which he hurriedly rubbed with a dirty fist. Catherine reached out the arm he'd pushed away a minute before, and he snuggled back against her, hiding his face against her shoulder.

"Now listen Paul, and you too, Benny," Catherine said, her response to Paul forming itself as she spoke. "There's a big difference between Pap and someone that belongs in jail." The children were very still. "Most people that go there did it to themselves, so going into debt's their own fault, and they got nobody else to blame. But it's not that way with Pap, because this ain't his fault."

Little as they were, the boys weren't stupid. Still looking for answers, Paul asked the inevitable question. "If it ain't Pap's fault he's in jail, then whose is it?"

The person responsible for her father's trouble suddenly flashed clear, as Catherine remembered scraps of conversation at the Fox which she hadn't credited at the time, if only because she was too proud to listen to gossip from the likes of John Skiles. Now they fell into a pattern.

Clearly, one name was behind every step in her father's difficulties, the final link apparent only yesterday, when the boys saw men cutting stones from the quarry and hauling them off towards the proposed railroad track, the local contract for which had been awarded to Will Carpenter. Catherine wanted to spit the name out like a toad, but something stopped her, as she sat pale and shaken, staring towards a gaggle of poultry in the lane.

Angry as she was, she knew that her father wouldn't want her to denounce the Squire to the boys, and she stood up. "Now Pap's away, we got to run things," she said irritably. "You hurry on and redd up in the barn. I got to look after Mama. And mind you don't come in till Peter gets home," she added. The boys stared at her. "Now get a move on," Catherine ordered, her hand on the door latch.

As though her anger were a disease and he'd caught it, Paul glared at her resentfully. "You think you're smart because you're big!" he said, "but all you are is big and mean and bossy!" He stuck out his tongue and ran towards the barn, Benny at his heels, while Catherine shrugged and went into the house.

But she was sorry for losing her temper the minute she opened the door, to find her mother slumped over the table, blood soaking onto her dress. Too frightened to gather her wits, Catherine flew back to the door. "Paul!" she screamed towards the barn. "Come here onct!"

It seemed like eternity before Benny ducked his head out of the stable door, then pulled it in again. Catherine called again. "Benny, call Paul! Mama's sick, and you have to go for help!"

At that, Paul slipped outside. "Why don't you do it yourself, bossy?"

Eventually, a frightened and repentant Catherine managed to pacify the boys and send them across the fields with instructions to fetch Lena Groff. As soon as they were gone, she hurried back inside, where she half dragged and half supported her mother to bed in the little room behind the kitchen.

16.

Before Peter got home, the house had been taken over by Lena Groff, a square and sixtyish woman with strong arms, capable hands, and a talent for coping with emergencies. Widowed for some years, old Mrs. Groff shared a nearby farm with her youngest son Daniel and his family. She was always ready to come away at a moment's notice, especially because she didn't get on with her daughter-in-law.

Mrs. Groff had assisted at innumerable births and was often consulted for lesser ailments because of her talent as a pow-wow, the gift passed to her from an uncle who'd lived with her family when she was a girl. When people came to her for help from stomach fever or wildfire or with a baby that was liver-grown, her answer was invariably, "Now, I don't know that this will help, but let me try, onct." Like most pow-wows, she was a sincerely religious woman and, like the Landises, went to the Mennonite church at Stumptown.

As he came down the lane, Peter was surprised at the quiet and wondered where the boys were, since ordinarily they'd have run out the lane to meet him. The day had turned overcast and drizzly, and even the poultry had taken shelter, like the five sheep huddled together under the barn overhang. The log house looked as forlorn as the animals, small and insignificant against the stone shell next to it. More and more surprised at the quiet, Peter paused outside to scrape his boots, just as Catherine opened the door, her face pale and frightened. Peter started to ask where the boys were, but she hushed him and drew him into the kitchen. "We got to talk quiet," she said. "Mama's sick."

Peter followed her to the fire, where Catherine whispered to him what had happened and explained that Lena Groff had insisted on sending the boys over to her daughter-in-law. "She said it wouldn't be right for them to be with Mama," she added, while she listened for sounds from the bedroom.

Peter shook his head. "They took Pap to *jail*?" he asked, not able to absorb Catherine's news.

"He couldn't raise Mr. Rees's money after the Carpenters took our quarry," she said bitterly. "And debtors go to jail."

Peter sat down heavily but instantly stood up again as the bedroom door opened, and the short, square figure of Lena Groff bustled into the kitchen. She nodded to Peter but shook her head and clicked her tongue when Catherine asked how her mother was.

"I won't say she's good," Mrs. Groff said, surveying the fireplace with a chunky hand on one hip. "Did you heat some water up, like I said?"

"It's not boiling yet," Catherine answered. "When it does, do you want me to fetch it into the bedroom?"

"What would I want it there for?" Lena Groff retorted impatiently. "Now be a good girl and shussle up your mam's teapot." She turned to inspect the young man. "You're Peter, ain't? Now just reach me that tutt, Peter," she said, indicating a paper sack on the far side of the table. "I'll get ready to make tea awhile."

She pulled some bundles from the bag, each wrapped in its

own piece of paper and tied with lapping yarn. After sniffing them one by one, she finally held one out as far as her arm could reach, squinting at the neat German label. "Your eyes are younger than mine," she remarked, handing it to Catherine. "Does that say pennyroyal?"

When Catherine nodded and asked what it was for, Lena Groff gave a significant look at Peter and turned her back to him, then stood on tiptoe and whispered in Catherine's ear: "Female complaints." Aloud, she said, "I picked this last summer, so it should have lots of strength left. Now, I can't say this will help your mam none, but I thought I'd try, onct."

She was heating the teapot when a sharp cry came from the bedroom. Mrs. Groff paused and shook her head. "I charmed over the knife I put under the bed—and it worked, too, but then the pain got bad as ever again. If the tea don't stop the baby from coming too soon, we'll have to fetch the doctor."

"If only Pap was home!" Catherine exclaimed, trying to keep from crying.

"Don't you worry on that," Mrs. Groff said, as she filled the teapot with herbs from her bundle. "He'll be here soon enough."

Peter and Catherine both looked at Mrs. Groff in surprise, while she lifted the kettle and poured water over the herbs. "There now," she said, before bothering to explain. "When I come over, I sent Daniel with word to Mart Mellinger about what's happened. After forty years of being deacon, I just guess he'll straighten things out. I'd like to know what a deacon's for," she added, "if it ain't to take care of folks in trouble."

"I never thought of that," Catherine said, musing, "only it wonders me that Pap didn't think to ask him."

"Your pap's proud and maybe too stiff-necked to ask for help where he should," Mrs. Groff retorted. "As for you, could be you don't know what church is about yet. That smells about right," she added, sniffing the tea. "Now, where do you hide your mam's cups?"

The tea ready, Mrs. Groff lifted the tray Catherine found for her, then paused, with a sharp look at Peter. "If I was you," she said, in more an order than a remark, "I'd think on stuff to do in the barn. The cattle need fed. As for you," she said, turning to Catherine, "the eggs must need gathered and the cow milked. There ain't a thing you can do in here. Besides," she added, balancing the tray in one hand while she opened the bedroom door with the other, "if the tea don't help, somebody got to be ready to ride to Lancaster and fetch the doctor. Now shussle, the both of you," she added, and disappeared into the bedroom.

The chores were long finished before Lena Groff could tell whether the tea would stop Elizabeth from premature labor. It was after dark when she came back into the kitchen, where Catherine was drawing uneven threads at the spinning wheel, too upset to concentrate on what she was doing. Peter sat at the table, fiddling over a broken toy he was half-heartedly trying to fix for Benny.

"It didn't help," Mrs. Groff announced, her voice matter-of-fact but her face grim and tired. "Your mam's got to have a doctor. I tried as hard as I could, but I can't do more."

Peter scrambled to his feet, grabbed a jacket from a peg by the door, and stuffed his arms into the sleeves confusedly, while Mrs. Groff gave hurried instructions on how to find the doctor's house.

"Dang it," Peter said under his breath and instantly glanced at Mrs. Groff to see if she'd heard him.

If she had she didn't comment. She looked at him sharply but not unkindly and said, "Now saddle the horse—and shussle!"

"Don't forget your hat!" Catherine called, as the door closed behind him, only to open again a second after. "It's raining," Peter said, grabbing his hat.

As the door closed again, Mrs. Groff sighed and shook her head. "It don't look good, not good at all," she commented, while Catherine studied her anxiously, the spinning a hopeless tangle.

"You're woman enough that I can tell you what I couldn't say to your brother," Lena Groff said wearily. "Let me just rest myself for a minute," she added, sinking into a chair and leaning her forehead against her hand. In a minute she raised her head and met Catherine's gaze.

"I can't find one sign that the baby's alive," she said. "Having a baby's hard enough in the best of times, but weak as your mam is, I can't see how she's going to make it through this."

Late the next afternoon Gideon came home, accompanied by Martin Mellinger, who'd spent the intervening time visiting the more affluent members of the Stumptown and Mellinger's congregations and, the money raised, paying Owen Rees and arranging for Gideon's release from the Lancaster jail.

Gaunt and shaken, Gideon arrived in time for the last earthly sight of his wife Elizabeth, who died after laboring to give birth to a dead infant, ultimately delivered with forceps by the doctor from Lancaster.

17.

It was several weeks since Elizabeth Buckwalter Landis and the baby born silent had been buried in the Siegrist family graveyard, just off the Provincial Road between the Fox and Enterprise. Reluctantly, Peter returned to Adam Wenger's because, as Gideon pointed out, Wenger was getting on and needed the help and, especially, because Peter had bargained to stay the year. When Peter protested that his father needed him for spring planting, Gideon answered that they could use the extra money.

There was no thought, however, that Catherine would go back to the Fox. From now on her duty was to take over for Elizabeth and look after Gideon and the boys. It was Catherine, now, who lived in the shadow of the new house and became almost hysterical when she found Benny and Paul climbing on the rafters.

Two more cows had calved, and besides preparing wool from the now naked sheep, Catherine had cheese and butter to make, more of it than usual to be sold, as another small way of raising cash against the pay Gideon still hadn't got from the Wilson estate. Instead of carrying it to the Fox, however, as her mother used to, Catherine sent Paul with it, her bitterness against the Carpenters too strong to let her go near the place.

If Catherine didn't go to the Fox, however, it came to her. The first emissary appeared one afternoon while she was heating milk, when she was interrupted by a timid knock at the door. First swinging the iron hinge to move the pot from the fire, she went to answer it and found Davy, looking more like a ragamuffin than ever. "I got lonesome," he said, "and I come to see you."

Catherine looked down at him without answering, her dislike of anything connected with the Fox making her wish he were a hundred miles away. Davy looked up at her, while his face shifted from enthusiasm to hurt when he didn't get the welcome he expected. "I'm sorry I come," he said, turning towards the lane. "Only I thought you was my friend."

He was a couple years older, but Davy wasn't any bigger than Paul, and he looked so pathetic as he tried to keep his mouth from quivering that Catherine was struck to the heart. She hurried to catch up with him and put a hand on his shoulder. "Don't go, Davy," Catherine said contritely. "I'm glad to see you."

She pulled him into the house and sat him at the table, overwhelming him with offers of food in her guilt for having taken her anger out on him. But Davy eyed her mistrustfully, as if, in one clumsy movement, Catherine had broken something fragile and could only try to put it together again. Still, ravenous as always, Davy ate the food she set out for him and thawed as his stomach filled. By the time he got to the crumb pie, he was once again the Davy she'd petted through the winter, and anxious as ever to sing Gumbo Jim's praises to her or the chimney piece.

"Gumbo's sad again," Davy said, "on account of his brother." Catherine paused over the milk she was stirring, and, carefully, so as not to show that she knew anything about

Cassius, asked Davy why. Instantly, Davy burst into a fabulous description of Cassius's escape, making it rival the adventures of Sinbad she'd heard from Eleanor. "But Gumbo says his brother works just as hard up in Canada as when he was a slave down South," Davy concluded. "Only now, if he don't keep up, he don't get nothing to eat. Gumbo says he might have saved hisself the trouble and stayed home."

"At least nobody owns him now," Catherine remarked, testing the milk on her wrist before she stirred in some dried membrane. More curious about goings on at the Fox than she'd have imagined an hour before, she pumped Davy for news. Mrs. Belcher, it seems, was doing duty as cook, gasping and wheezing over the fire and burning the meat whenever she couldn't sigh, to the protests of Mrs. Carpenter and the customers. "It sure ain't like when you was there," Davy said wistfully.

"The bread's real good, though," he added. "Miss Martha and that funny old lady do that — but their pies ain't as good as yours," he added loyally.

"What old lady?" Catherine asked, looking up from the kettle. "I didn't hear about any visitors."

Davy stretched back his shoulders, full of pride that he had some news, for once not preempted by John Skiles, and told her about Sophia Passmore's invasion of the Fox. "She's bossy," he added, "only, she ain't as mean as old lady Carpenter."

"That's no way to talk, Davy," Catherine said, much as she shared his judgment.

Davy hunched his shoulders. "She ain't mean, anyhow," he corrected himself, adding, "the new one's real queer and fussy, but she don't yell at me. And Wednesday she gave me a penny for helping her."

Catherine bit her tongue to keep from saying that the visitor could hardly be Penelope Carpenter's sister. Instead, she commented, "That must be the aunt Eleanor thinks so much on, ain't?" Davy nodded, and Catherine asked what she was like, curious how the strange lady came to be in Davy's good graces.

"Well, she has a long nose," Davy said, struggling for ways

to describe her, "and she wears a big green bonnet." He wrinkled his nose in puzzlement before adding triumphantly, "And she ain't hardly bigger than I am!"

By now Catherine had poured the milk and put it aside to settle. "I got to get on with my chores, Davy," she said, well aware that, as usual, he must have slipped off to see her when he had work to do. "You'd better run on home, or you'll be in trouble."

Davy scrambled to his feet. "I forgot what I come over for," he said. "Gumbo and everyone, they said I was to tell you how sorry they are about your mam. Me too," he added before he made for the door and ran off towards the Fox.

Catherine wiped her eyes as she watched Davy out the lane, then resolutely blew her nose and went to gather the eggs. But when she got to the chicken coop, she set down her egg basket and had a good cry.

Catherine's next reminder of the Fox came a few days later as she was behind the house working at the cold frame, placed where it caught the south sun and gave a good start to the bedding plants. Hearing bells in the distance, she wondered idly if someone was taking a Conestoga to Adam Wenger's for repair, when, to her surprise, it turned in the lane.

Putting down her trowel, Catherine got up and looked around the corner to see a handsomely groomed team, a lanky redhead walking beside it. As the blood rushed to her face, she hurriedly ducked back out of sight to compose herself. Since she'd been home, her mother's death and her father's problems had kept her from thinking much about Jake Good, who seemed to belong to a part of her life gone as completely as the family's dreams of the new house. Seeing him now, she hastily rubbed the dirt from her hands and felt her hair to be sure it was in place. It wasn't till the bells stopped beside the house and she heard Jake calling that she stepped into sight, as though she'd just that moment gotten up from her work.

"I didn't think anybody was home," Jake said, looking surprisingly shy.

"Pap and the boys are out harrowing," Catherine answered, equally at a loss. "I've been redding up the cold frame," she added, for loss of anything else to say.

Jake fidgeted with his whip handle. "I was just down this way," he said, "so I thought maybe I'd stop by and tell you I'm sorry about your mam. I really am, Katlie," he added, meeting her eyes and blushing. He hurried on, "I didn't even stop at the Fox, when I knew you weren't there no more."

"How'd you hear that?" Catherine asked, surprised.

"Word gets around," Jake answered, shuffling his feet. Then, seeing her puzzled look, he again met her eyes. "My pap heard it from the bishop, and he heard it from Mart Mellinger at spring conference. And that's how I heard," Jake finished lamely.

"Oh," Catherine said, as though it were all perfectly clear. The color again rose in his face and, studying his whip handle, Jake blurted, "The bishop heard I might be interested in knowing what happened, that's all."

Catherine turned away. "Then you must know the rest of what happened, too," she said bitterly. When Jake didn't answer, she went on, "By now everyone knows how Pap got put in jail for debt. You heard that, too, didn't you?"

"I heard about it," Jake admitted reluctantly. More confidently, he added, "Only I heard it wasn't his fault, either. From the way your pap got messed around with on that land he sold, nobody can hold what happened against him."

She didn't answer, and both were silent till Catherine said, "I thought you weren't coming down this way any more, now that planting's started."

Her shift in manner seemed to relieve Jake. "If you're not at the Fox, and you're not going to parties or frolics, how else can I get to see you?" he asked, falling into the droll way of talking she'd come to expect from him.

"Besides," he continued more seriously, "Hank Mummaw asked me to see off this load to Pittsburgh for him, and I couldn't see my way to turning him down, when I had a reason

137

for getting down this way besides."

Thinking of the Squire's interest in money, Catherine said sarcastically, "If you get paid enough, I guess you can leave farm work whenever you feel like it."

Surprised at her tone, Jake defended himself. "I got two brothers," he said. "And there's nothing wrong with making money by honest work." He paused, studying her face. In a lower voice, he added, "I got enough saved now, Katlie, and I'm looking around for a farm. Land's high around here, and my pap's place isn't big enough to cut in half, but one of my cousins is checking out prices in Canada. If they're good, I might even move up there, where Bishop Eby's brother lives."

Catherine stared at him dumbly, stunned to realize that Jake might soon be gone as completely as her mother.

Meantime, Jake was watching her anxiously, waiting for her reaction. For a long minute she couldn't say anything. To her embarrassment, tears came to her eyes, and she turned away to wipe them. Finally, she made herself speak, but only after Jake prompted, "What do you think, Katlie? It's a good idea, ain't?"

"I know you'll do real well wherever you find one," Catherine said at last, the insincerity in her voice contradicting her words.

Noticing only the words, Jake relaxed into a smile. "I wanted to know what your pap thought of it," he said cheerfully. "That's another reason I stopped. Where'd you say he was?"

With constrained politeness, Catherine directed him to the field where Gideon was working and watched as he disappeared up the path, turning back once to wave to her. She started to wave back and stopped, overcome with the sense of how hard it was to say goodbye to Jake Good.

Hastily finishing her work at the cold frame, she went into the kitchen, tied on her bonnet, and set off to visit Lena Groff. By the time she got back an hour and a half later, Jake and his wagon were gone.

Gideon didn't mention Jake's visit, but that was hardly surprising, as quiet as he'd been since Elizabeth's death, so quiet, in fact, that Catherine sometimes fancied that some stranger had changed places with her father. This man looked like the old Gideon and was as careful as the real one about managing the farm, but he spoke as little as he could and sometimes even snapped at the boys instead of teasing them out of stupidities or correcting them with a brisk, "Now straighten up there!" the way the old Gideon used to.

During silent grace before meals, Gideon's head stayed bowed so long that the boys, Benny especially, fidgeted and eyed the food getting cold on the platters. They ate their food silently, too, with no jokes now about Patience Slack or John Skiles to go with the pie or the coffee, which Catherine poured for her father as her mother always had before.

She'd gotten so used to silent meals that Catherine was surprised a few days later when her father called her back as she was clearing the table. "Sit down onct," Gideon said. "I got something I want to talk to you about."

Obediently, Catherine put the stack of dishes in the dry sink and sat down at the table, first sending the boys out to play.

Her father wasn't in a hurry to begin and blew over the coffee in his saucer, drank, and set it down beside the cup stand. Meditatively pushing some crumbs back and forth with his finger, he finally said, "I'm thinking on selling."

Catherine stared at him wide-eyed. "You mean selling the farm?" she asked incredulously. Still pushing the crumbs as if they held extraordinary interest, Gideon nodded, and Catherine blurted, "Why would you want to do that?"

"To pay off my debts," Gideon replied, meeting his daughter's eyes. Catherine was confused, knowing that the debt to Owen Rees had been settled and assuming that the family was over the worst. But she hadn't calculated on her father's pride.

"I know Rees got his pay," Gideon went on, "but I wasn't the one that paid him. After all, Brother Martin's been deacon long enough that when he asks for money, nobody hides his pocketbook." Gideon paused and passed a hand over his forehead.

"Katlie," he said in a weary voice, "you know better than to think it's right for us to take charity. The brothers and sisters pitched in and helped me out of a bind, but I'm going to pay them back, every red cent, and if I got to sell the farm, well, I'll just have to."

She knew better than to contradict her father, but Catherine couldn't stop herself. "You can't!" she exclaimed. "You'll pay them back when the Wilson estate gets settled!"

Instead of putting her in her place, Gideon raised an ironic eyebrow. "When?" he asked. "It's been months already, and all we got from it so far is the quarry taken. From the look of things, the Squire's not in a hurry to settle anything."

Catherine's anger welled up at the reminder of Will Carpenter's role in their troubles. "Where would we move," she asked bitterly, "to Lancaster and sweep chimneys?"

"Is that kind of work too low for a man that's been to jail?" her father retorted. Catherine hadn't often seen him angry, and she flinched at the passion in his voice as he continued, "Why not Ohio? Or why not Canada? That's where other slaves go, if they can get out from under!" Hearing himself, he dropped his voice and again fixed his eyes on the scattered crumbs.

"This place should fetch a good enough price to pay back the brothers and sisters," he concluded, pushing himself up from the table. At the door he paused and added, "You better not say anything to the boys just yet."

As she poured water into the basin and started the dishes, Catherine was in a turmoil. Too much was happening too fast, the life she knew melting around her like onion snow. Clumsily, she dropped a plate which smashed at her feet. "Dang it!" she exclaimed, stamping her foot in frustration.

18.

The Fox continued to exert its influence on Catherine. As carefully as she avoided going there, Will Carpenter's part in the disintegration of her family cast a shadow as sharp as the one made by the shell of the new house when she stepped outside in the morning. Though she tried to forget her months at the Fox, memories persisted, perhaps of Mrs. Belcher wheezing and trying to sigh, perhaps of Gumbo Jim huddling over the kitchen fire. If nothing else, Davy's visit at least prodded her into separating the workers from the masters, after her initial revulsion from anything to do with the inn on the Old Road. She remained adamant, however, in her condemnation of the Carpenter clan, from the unscrupulous Squire through the wily lawyer son to the bossy and pretentious wife, with the daughters of the house thrown in for good measure.

Even working in the garden didn't drain her resentment. Enclosed by pickets to keep out the chickens, geese, and guineas who pecked at gravel and seed indiscriminately, the garden was laid out like a cross, with a rose bush where the paths intersected. Elizabeth had especially enjoyed working there, screened from the barn by the currant bushes along the side. Her private place, she called it, and as good as church when she needed to get her thoughts in order. But while she readied it for planting, Catherine only felt the effort of wielding the heavy rake in one mechanical movement after another, and she left the garden the moment she thought of something else to do.

As Easter approached, she felt more and more like leaving the house and the garden on any pretext, to look for early shoots of poke or hunt for the nest a cluck had hidden. She forgot one outdoor ritual till Gideon reminded her, with the remark that he wouldn't turn up his nose to a mess of dandelions.

The yard by the kitchen was badly trampled, and to avoid being near the new house, Catherine took her knife and kettle into the orchard. A few trees showed sprigs of bloom, but, weather holding, it would be another week before the trees came into flower.

She was probing for a root, when she thought she heard a voice. Catherine raised her head and listened, only to hear, more distinctly this time, someone calling, "Yoo hoo! Is anybody home?" Tossing a dandelion into her kettle, she stood up and called back, wondering who her visitor was.

The owner of the voice appeared at the fringe of the orchard, paused to peer through the trees, and briskly made her way towards Catherine. "Oh, there you are," said the strange lady in the green bonnet. "When you weren't in the house, I came looking for you." The woman obviously hadn't come from a farm. Tiny as she was, she carried herself with distinction and was simply but elegantly dressed, down to the grey gloves buttoned at the wrist, though Catherine hadn't heard a carriage or even a horse.

Instead of introducing herself, she peered into Catherine's kettle. "Gathering dandelions, I see," she remarked, and, without so much as a by-your-leave, reached into Catherine's kettle and helped herself to a leaf, which she nibbled experimentally.

"It's bitter," she said, "but I suppose you people are used to that."

Catherine drew in her breath, guessing who the lady was from Davy's description. "I wonder if I could trouble you for something to drink?" Sophia Passmore asked pleasantly. "I've had a good walk from the Fox. Now, I just wonder if you might have some buttermilk on hand. A drink of buttermilk is just what I could fancy."

No matter what her feelings were, Catherine couldn't refuse a request for food or drink. "There's some in the cellar," she said curtly and, kettle in hand, led the way towards the house.

"My," Miss Passmore said as they emerged from the trees to a clear view of the new house. "That will be a handsome building when it's finished."

"It's not likely to be, now," Catherine said, and hurried to the kitchen, where she seated her genteel guest at the table and went to fetch a crock from the cellar.

"Thank you, dear," Miss Passmore said, taking the tumbler Catherine poured for her and sipping it with relish. "I thought you'd have some on hand, from the butter you sell the Fox. And fine butter it is, too," she added. "It's a pity you're not cooking there any more. Since I arrived I haven't heard anything but sighs that you left."

"Mama taught me to cook," Catherine answered proudly.

"I know, dear. I've heard what a fine woman she was," commented Miss Passmore. Without warning, she reached over and took Catherine's hand. "I know how hard it is to lose a mother," she added with a sympathetic squeeze.

Her movement caught Catherine off guard. Moreover, her hand caught in Miss Passmore's, Catherine was trapped. "Please sit down," her visitor said, holding her firmly. "I've been looking forward to a chat with you."

Catherine sat down abruptly in the chair Miss Passmore indicated, only to find herself being scrutinized by a pair of sharp brown eyes.

"I've wondered what you were like," the older woman said,

"as much as I've heard about you. You're prettier than I expected," she added meditatively.

Catherine bristled. "Why shouldn't I be pretty?" she asked indignantly. "Looks don't come from being rich."

"Oh, it's not that, dear," Miss Passmore instantly responded. She paused, and Catherine looked at her inquiringly. "I really shouldn't say any more," she said. "I told Eleanor I wouldn't."

Her curiosity aroused, Catherine rose like a fish to Sophia Passmore's bait. "Say anything about what?" she asked.

"I shouldn't tell you, of course. But now that I've let that much slip," Miss Passmore said, "I suppose I might as well go on." She picked up the empty tumbler and turned it in her hands, as though she were studying messages in the milk residue. Finally setting it down, she met Catherine's gaze.

"I really came to see you today to find out why you haven't been to see Eleanor," she said. "She can't understand why you didn't visit her in her trouble. And to be honest," she added, "neither can I."

Catherine's mouth opened in astonishment. Surely this meddling old woman knew her reasons for avoiding the Fox, but there she sat, demurely telling Catherine what to do. Miss Passmore's penetrating eyes never left her face, and realizing that she had to explain herself, Catherine finally blurted, "The Squire cheated my pap. He might as well have stolen the farm outright, only he was smart enough to get the law to do it for him. And that's why I don't want to see him, or Eleanor either."

"I thought it must be that," Sophia Passmore said, fingering her chin and tapping her lips meditatively. "I understand," she said at last, "—though, of course, I think you're wrong." Like a rebellious child forced to wait for dismissal, Catherine clenched her teeth, as Miss Passmore continued, "No matter how you feel about the Squire," she said slowly, "I want you to keep in mind that Eleanor didn't choose to be her father's daughter, and your church must teach that it's wrong to visit the father's sins on the children. I certainly didn't come here to defend Will Carpenter or anything he's done. Only remember, dear, you have to judge his daughter as a separate person—and she did count on your friendship."

When Catherine didn't answer, Miss Passmore sighed and rose from the table. "I have to be getting back," she said, adjusting her bonnet and smoothing her gloves.

"How is she?" Catherine asked suddenly.

"Not well," Miss Passmore replied, pausing and shaking her head. "She's not in any danger for now—but I can't see into the future, low as her spirits are." Animated once more, she offered to pay for the buttermilk, and on Catherine's refusal, disappeared into the April morning as suddenly as she'd come, leaving Catherine with mixed feelings of resentment and, in spite of herself, guilt.

Later, as Catherine dished up supper, Gideon casually inquired who her visitor had been. "What did she want?" he asked when Catherine told him.

"She wants me to visit Eleanor Johns," Catherine replied, putting the platter of blanched dandelion in front of her father, who prayed less lengthily than he usually had lately and took a good-sized helping, including plenty of dressing and sliced eggs.

Gideon passed the platter to the boys and barely stopped Benny from dishing the rest onto his own plate. "Here now!" Gideon said. "If you're going to fress like a wootzie, we'll send you out to eat with the rest of the pigs." Paul tittered but was careful not to take more than his share. "You got to think of other people," Gideon added to the smaller boy, before he turned back to his own plate.

The platter was making a second round before Gideon again took up the subject of Miss Passmore's visit. "Any special reason she thinks you should visit Mrs. Johns?" he asked his daughter, who, after serving the others, was only now eating.

"She says she counted on me to be her friend," Catherine answered reluctantly.

"That so?" Gideon remarked. Thoughtfully, he took a bite of bread, a frown playing across his forehead.

"Can I have more now?" Benny asked, and Catherine dished another portion onto his plate. It was the first fresh vegetable he'd had since fall, and both boys were ravenous.

Gideon, however, had satisfied his appetite and, to Catherine's discomfort, asked why Eleanor Johns counted on her as a friend.

"We were together a lot," Catherine said evasively, simultaneously realizing that she'd used too much vinegar in the dressing. Her own hunger had left, and she toyed with the dandelion on her plate, not wanting to elaborate. Finally, she put down her fork. "She asked me to be her friend," Catherine said. "I didn't want to, but she made me promise — and I did," she finished lamely, before adding vehemently, "Only that was before I found out how awful the Carpenters are. I don't like her now, or any of them!"

"Can I have some pie?" Benny asked.

"Hush up and wait on your sister," Gideon commanded, but Catherine jumped up and hurried to the pie safe, happy for an excuse to break off the conversation. But when she put the pie on the table, her father had a word to add.

"A promise is a promise," he said. "You better go see her tomorrow. And finish your plate," he added, "or we won't have a clear day tomorrow."

Catherine had never swallowed anything so bitter in her life.

19.

The next morning Catherine kept herself very busy, cleaning the house from top to bottom. Her hair tucked under a dust cap, she washed windows, scrubbed floors, and hauled rugs out to the clothesline. Ordinarily she'd have asked the boys to beat them, but today she thwacked them with her broom till the dust flew and stuck to her face, giving her a gypsyish look, in spite of the surprising blue eyes. Over dinner she was grumpy and rebuked the boys, drawing a long look from her father, who quietly asked when she was planning on going to the Fox.

"I got to finish the cleaning," she replied, knowing as well as he did that her sudden attack on dirt and grime was an excuse for postponing that very question.

"You'd better make it this afternoon," Gideon said in what Catherine knew was an order. "If you get home late, we can scramble up supper here, but I don't much like you walking near the Old Road after dark. And while you're at it," he added, "how about taking your little brother along?"

"Can I see the eagle?" Benny piped up excitedly.

Catherine nodded, knowing that she couldn't escape her interview with Eleanor Johns, though the thought of it made her stomach churn.

"Why can't I go, Pap?" Paul asked, pushing out his lower lip.

"I need you here," Gideon answered. "The work we're doing, your brother would be underfoot, but you're big enough to be a help."

Pacified, Paul looked at his brother condescendingly. "Babies don't work and do hard things," he said smugly.

After dinner Catherine worked more and more slowly, having nonetheless fixed the time for her visit for after the dinner hour at the Fox, in the fervent hope that she'd see as few people as possible. Finally, she had no choice but to call Benny and make both of them as spruce as she could, then, unwillingly, set off towards the Fox.

Benny was in high good spirits and scampered off in all directions, while his sister trudged doggedly along the dirt road. The eagle he wanted to visit was on his mind, and he was having a fine time watching for birds that reminded him of it.

They were midway in their walk when he called to Catherine excitedly, "Look up there! There's a whole bunch of them!" Catherine looked up from the road she'd been studying yard by yard.

Benny was pointing to the sky, where, sure enough, a number of big birds were circling and dropping down one by one behind a rise. "We can see them up close!" Benny cried, and before Catherine could stop him, he was off across the field.

"Wait, Benny!" Catherine called. "Those aren't eagles!"

"Are so!" he shouted back and disappeared over the rise. Afraid of losing him, Catherine hitched up her skirts and ran after him.

The field ended just over the hill, its margin marked by a snake fence, which zigzagged crazily between cropland and wilderness. Benny was standing a short distance from a row of birds sitting along the upper rail and staring back with beady eyes, their dark bodies contrasting starkly with the obscene nakedness of their long hunched necks and their purplish faces.

Catherine had known what to expect from the fringes on their wings, but she still shuddered when she saw them, several perched with one wing extended, as if to say, This prey is ours. Benny stared at them, his eyes round. "I ain't never seen turkey buzzards up close before," he whispered. "They're *ugly*!"

"Don't go closer," Catherine said, putting her hands on his shoulders. "They've found something to eat, and they'll think we want it."

"Pee yew!" Benny said and pinched his nose, while Catherine stood on tiptoe and stretched to see over the weeds by the fence, where, as they watched, two of the birds hopped down clumsily.

"I think it's a deer," Catherine said, and started to gag. "Come on, Benny," she said, trying to keep from retching. Subdued, her brother followed her back to the road and stayed beside her the rest of the way to the Fox.

All the way, Catherine debated how she could visit Eleanor without seeing the rest of the family. She'd have been happier not to see anyone, but the best she could think of was to slip in and send word upstairs that she'd arrived. Accordingly, when they got to the inn, Benny ran across the courtyard to visit the eagle, while she went to the kitchen.

Like the one to the taproom, the kitchen door stood open to catch the mild afternoon air. Hearing the clatter of dishes, Catherine guessed that Mrs. Belcher was washing up from dinner. She paused on the doorstep, called, and walked in.

The room looked smaller than she remembered, perhaps because of Mrs. Belcher, who, if possible, looked fatter than ever. Sleeves pushed up and fat quivering on her forearms, the new cook was scrubbing at a pile of dishes.

"Well, look what the cat dragged in," she wheezed when she saw Catherine. She didn't seem pleased and asked the girl what her business was. When Catherine explained, Mrs. Belcher suddenly broke into a smile that buried her eyes and began to welcome the guest effusively. "It hit me that could be you come to get your job back," she explained. "Do you mind just giving me a hand here awhile?"—and she thrust a dishtowel at Catherine. "The minute the dishes is done, I'll run up the steps with word you're come."

In spite of Mrs. Belcher's frequent assurances that she used to be only a slip of a thing, Catherine doubted if the cook had ever run anywhere in her life. Still, not wanting to offend her, Catherine took the dishtowel and helped with the wiping, silently rubbing off bits of food and streaks of gravy missed in the haphazard washing. Politely, she inquired after Mrs. Belcher's asthma.

"Bless your heart," the cook panted in reply, "I'm wonderful better now." When Catherine asked whether she was taking new medicine, she looked at the girl slyly. "Best kind of all," she answered, "and I'll say it done wonders for me." Lowering her voice, she wheezed in Catherine's ear, "The duchess upstairs was stuck for a cook when you left, and I just told her my asthma was too bad unless I got a dollar ten a week. I hardly been sick a bit ever since," she concluded triumphantly, punctuating her explanation with a wink at the astonished Catherine.

Catherine was too shocked to comment, especially when she remembered how often she'd done double duty when Mrs. Belcher sent word she was too sick to work. Noticing the girl's expression and remembering too late that she might not be pleased, Mrs. Belcher made a quick shift into wheedling self-justification.

"A body's got to look after hisself in this world," she said defensively, "or there ain't nobody else is going to do it for them. It ain't like I have the chance to get ahead and make money, like Mrs. Slack."

"You mean Patience Slack that used to work here?" Catherine asked in surprise.

"Her and nobody else is who I mean," declared Mrs. Belcher. "Why, now she's as fancy as anybody in Lancaster, dresses just as good—and wears rings, too—even if she wasn't no better than she should of been, the ways she got them. Mrs. Slack knew how to get ahead, all right. I could of too, when I was your age and just a slip of a thing, only now I ain't got the shape for it, more's the pity."

Catherine wouldn't listen to more. Putting down the cup she'd been drying, she told Mrs. Belcher that her time was short and she had to let Mrs. Johns know she'd come.

"All right, then, if I got to face them steps," Mrs. Belcher wheezed back. "Just give me a minute to catch my breath." She dried her hands and stood panting, then let out a sigh that sounded like a winded horse. "There now," she said, smiled with satisfaction, and waddled up the steps, returning in a few minutes to say that Eleanor was waiting for her.

Relief at escaping from Mrs. Belcher hurried Catherine out of the kitchen. Before she knew it, she was in the dining room of the Fox and being hugged frantically by Eleanor Johns, while she submitted stiffly.

"It's so wonderful to see you!" Eleanor exclaimed. "Aunt Sophie said you'd come, but I waited, and when you didn't, I thought you didn't like me anymore. But it's all right now, because we're still friends. Why did you wait so long?"

"We had trouble at home," Catherine answered evasively, wondering that Eleanor hadn't yet mentioned her mother's death.

"Let me look at you," Eleanor bubbled, stepping back and surveying Catherine at arm's length. "You haven't changed. You're the same wonderful, pretty Catherine as ever!"

But if Eleanor didn't see changes in Catherine, Catherine saw them in Eleanor. Though it was afternoon, she was wearing a saffron dressing gown buttoned high around her neck. The sleeves were long, but with her arms extended, they'd pulled back from her wrists to show a set of barely-healed scars. The most remarkable change, however, was in the pinched face, which seemed to be taken up with a pair of eyes looking at her hungrily out of dark sockets. In spite of herself, Catherine felt a

151

surge of pity, as though she'd found a pretty butterfly with its wings tattered and the colors rubbed off.

Feeling more constrained than ever, Catherine let herself be led through the dining room and into the parlor. "We could visit here," Eleanor remarked, her eyes flitting over the heavy furniture and silent piano and fixing on the steadily ticking grandfather clock. "It would be more proper, only I hoped you'd come to my room instead. Nobody will bother us there. Besides," she added, with an edge of peevishness, "I can't stand that horrible clock!

"It's a lesson, Papa says," she continued, answering Catherine's look. "Always-be-ahead-of-time, always-be-ahead-of-time,"she intoned, matching her words to the ticking of the clock. "Playing the piano, I went wild from it, only it's worse now." She broke off. "Come," she ordered brightly, and led the way up the central staircase, Catherine reluctantly at her heels, her fingers crossed that she wouldn't see any more Carpenters.

Like most of the rooms not delegated to servants, Eleanor's had its own fireplace and comfortable furniture, including an upholstered chair, while the walls were papered prettily. Catherine hadn't seen it before, and she looked around curiously.

"You're the guest, and you have to sit in the chair," Eleanor said, pushing Catherine into it. "Do as I say," she ordered, as Catherine protested. "I'll take the bed. It's more comfortable anyway, when I sit in that chair all day."

The gush of words stopped suddenly, succeeded by an awkward silence, Catherine in no mood for light chitchat with the Squire's daughter, and Eleanor watching her expectantly from her pathetically circled eyes. Perched on the high bed, Eleanor's feet dangled childishly above the carpet, making a grotesque contrast with the drawn face, which could have belonged to an ailing middle-aged woman—to her own mother, Catherine realized with a shock. Moreover, the extravagant welcome seemed to have used up Eleanor's strength, and her eyes pleaded with Catherine to return her welcome.

Giving in to her conscience, Catherine said, "I couldn't come because Mama was sick." Surprised, Eleanor asked if she was better. "She's dead," Catherine answered, the spiteful pleasure she felt as Eleanor winced succeeded instantly by a rush of guilt for deliberately hurting the sick girl. After all, even if Eleanor was the Squire's daughter, she'd never been mean — thoughtless and self-centered, but never, Catherine knew, by intention. Catherine could have bitten out her tongue the moment her words snaked out.

Contritely, she leaned forward and asked how Eleanor had been. Eleanor didn't seem to realize the meanness she'd committed and smiled with relief. Even so, her answer was less than straightforward.

"I haven't been at all well since that man attacked me in the field," she said.

The answer made Catherine's head spin, knowing as she did that no such man existed, except in Will Carpenter's scheme to cover up Eleanor's attempted suicide. Eleanor was burbling on about how frightened she'd been, the razor open in the man's hand, when she stopped, seeing Catherine's disbelief. "You know, don't you?" she asked, suddenly dropping her affectation.

Catherine nodded. "Jim told Martha and me when it happened," she answered, as embarrassed as if she'd been the one caught lying.

"You haven't told, have you?" Eleanor cried, her voice rising in panic. She leaned forward, swaying a bit and desperate to hear Catherine's assurance that her reputation was safe. The orange-yellow of her dressing gown would have highlighted the richness of the old Eleanor's complexion, but now, as she strained towards Catherine, the color only emphasized her resemblance to a skull.

"No," Catherine answered. "I'd have told Pap, but he's been upset about Mama — and everything else. Oh, Eleanor!" she blurted. "Killing himself is the worst thing anyone can do. Why did you try something so awful!"

The corners of Eleanor's mouth drew back into a mirthless

grin. "Don't you know that, too, along with everything else?" she asked bitterly. Catherine shook her head while Eleanor studied her face.

"I believe you," Eleanor said finally. Belligerent as she was a moment before, her voice suddenly became matter-of-fact. "I'll be lucky if the whole countryside doesn't know pretty soon," she said almost jauntily. "I'm going to have a baby."

Though such a possibility had crossed Catherine's mind, knowing as she did of Eleanor's intimacy with Nicholas McMaster, she was too shocked to say anything but "Oh, Eleanor!"

Eleanor studied her fingernails as though she'd forgotten Catherine was there. After a moment Catherine spoke again, instinctively lowering her voice. "He's going to marry you, ain't so?" Still studying her fingernails, Eleanor shook her head. "But you told me you're divorced now and can get married again," Catherine said in astonishment.

Wearily, Eleanor put her hand on the bedcover, as though she were too weak to sit without a support. "I know now why they call him Old Nick," she said simply. "He won't marry me."

Catherine's heart went out to her. She jumped from her chair and joined Eleanor on the bed. "I'm so awful, awful sorry," she said, putting an arm around Eleanor's shoulder, her anger with the Squire forgotten in her compassion.

"I knew I could count on you when you told me you'd be my friend," Eleanor said, relief in her voice.

Catherine stiffened, remembering the unfortunate promises Eleanor had extorted from her, which, at the time, she'd seen no way of avoiding. "Anyhow, I came to see you," she answered evasively.

Absorbed in her own problems, Eleanor ignored her. "The worst of it is," she said, as though to herself, "I've wanted a baby so much. I want to hug him and kiss him and dress him and undress him and buy him pretty clothes.

"And I don't have to buy them, either," she added, turning

to Catherine. "I have a whole chestful of things I got ready for Alexander—the prettiest little dresses. Just the lace for the christening gown cost twenty dollars—but he didn't live long enough to wear it."

She fell into one of the silences Catherine remembered from her visits by the kitchen fire. Catherine waited, but though Eleanor was beside her, she might have been a hundred miles away. Knowing from experience that she might stay in her reverie indefinitely, Catherine made an effort to recall her. "If Mr. McMaster won't marry you, what are you going to do about the baby?" she asked.

Eleanor wriggled impatiently and slid from the bed. Restlessly, she flitted to a little table and began rearranging a clutter of bottles, needlework, and bric-a-brac. "Aunt Sophie and my brother are looking after things," she said, her back to Catherine. "Aunt Sophie and I are going to Bedford Springs. I'll be respectably married to a Philadelphia sea captain—for now."

Still without looking at Catherine, she picked up a figurine and carried it to the window, where she studied it intently and began to dust it with her handkerchief, tracing the details through the cloth with her finger. "Have you heard of Bedford Springs?" she asked. "It's on the way to Pittsburgh, and it's very expensive. Only the very best people go there. I'm to drink the waters and benefit from the healthful mountain air." She wheeled towards the bed, the figurine clutched in her hand. "Oh, Catherine," she wailed. "They say I can't keep the baby! You've got to help me!"

Catherine looked at Eleanor in astonishment, the realization dawning on her that she'd been trapped again, though she didn't know how or what the trap was, and her next words bristled with defensiveness. "I don't know what you think I could do," she said. "It looks to me like everything's taken care of already."

"No!" Eleanor cried. Hurriedly replacing the figurine, she ran to the bed and seized Catherine's hands. "Don't you see?" she asked, her voice rising hysterically. "I have to give my baby

155

away. I have to know he has a good home!"

Catherine's hostility to the Carpenters rushed back. "You want me to take your baby and raise it like it was mine," she said flatly.

"Of course!" Eleanor said, squeezing her hands and beaming at her. "Who else do I like enough to give my baby to?—I can't give him to a stranger. It's the perfect plan!"

"Perfect for you, maybe," Catherine said slowly, trying to pull her hands from Eleanor's, "only I can't say that it is for me."

"No, listen!" Eleanor demanded. "It wouldn't be for nothing! Papa will pay you!"

"With the money he stole from my pap?" Catherine asked venomously.

Eleanor released Catherine's hands and stepped back. "You're wrong about Papa," she said. "He wouldn't do that." As though she'd resolved the problem, she returned to her subject.

"I thought and thought about how I could know he'd have a good home," she said, "but all I could think of was you and your little brothers. And then I remembered you promising to be my friend. I knew you wouldn't go back on your word." She stopped, seeing the hostility in Catherine's face. "You are still my friend, aren't you?" she asked hesitantly.

Catherine's head was throbbing. "I don't know," she answered. With a surge of relief, she noticed that the light was fading, and she had to get home.

"You'll do it, won't you?" Eleanor asked in a frightened voice as Catherine made for the door. Her hand on the latch, Catherine turned back. "I got the headache too bad to think about it now," she said, and slipped from the room.

20.

Catherine couldn't escape from the Fox, however, without running the gauntlet of the rest of household. At the foot of the stairs, a glance assured her that the door of the Squire's office was closed. Relieved to that extent, she slipped through the parlor and past the clock, which she glanced at apprehensively on her way towards the kitchen steps, pleased that so far her way was clear. But she wasn't so lucky in the dining room, which she'd no sooner stepped into than Will Carpenter's other daughter rose from where she was examining a pile of silverware.

"Mrs. Belcher said you were here," Martha Carpenter said, her bulldog face looking like a feminized version of the Squire's. "I hoped I'd catch you."

"I have to leave now," Catherine said, seizing on the first thing she could think of to avoid another round of pressure from the Carpenter clan. "Pap said I was to be home by dark."

Martha's face was expressionless as she held out her hand. "I heard about your mother," she said, "and I wanted you to know I'm sorry."

Surprised and moved in spite of herself, Catherine raised a tentative hand in response and received a squeeze from Martha's capable fingers. "I know things have been hard for you lately," Martha said.

"We've had bad times," Catherine answered simply, wondering how much Martha Carpenter knew about her father's role in the Landises' difficulties.

But Martha's next words anticipated Catherine's silent question. "I know about everything," she said, emphasizing the last word. "I can't help what my father does — or my sister either, for that matter. But I can still be sorry."

Releasing Catherine's hand, she turned back to the pile of tableware, which she continued to sort and inspect methodically, while she went on, "I've thought of leaving, often enough, and of moving to Philadelphia, perhaps, or New York, where I could live my own life."

"Why don't you?" Catherine asked, as fascinated as if she were listening to a speaking stone.

"Mostly because, when I think about it, I'm not sure that running away changes anything," Martha answered. "People have to take me or leave me as I am. I'd be the same person no matter where I went," she finished, clamping her mouth.

She appeared to have had her say, and Catherine was about to make her escape, when Martha fired a question at her. "What are you going to do about Eleanor?" she asked, scrutinizing a dented spoon.

Taken by surprise, Catherine could only stutter, "I — I don't know. I haven't had time to think about it yet."

"You should know, anyway, that it was Aunt Sophie's idea," Martha said, in her businesslike voice. "She put Eleanor up to asking you, after she heard you were friends. My sister hadn't the brains to think of it for herself," she added, looking up. "I had nothing to do with it, that's all."

The room suddenly felt so stuffy that Catherine had to get out. "Thank you," she said, not sure that she meant it. "I really got to go home." Martha nodded and went back to her silver.

"Whatever you decide, good luck," were her parting words, as Catherine plunged down the kitchen steps.

Luckily, Mrs. Belcher wasn't in the kitchen, and Catherine hurried outside, where she looked towards the lean-to holding the hunched eagle. It would be dark soon, but Benny wasn't to be seen. Hesitantly, Catherine walked across the courtyard towards the stable, calling him.

The top of the double door was open, and when she got closer, Benny's eyes popped into view, peering out at her. "Here I am, Katlie!" he called. Davy's head appeared beside his and, making a pyramid in the dusk, the tall figure of Gumbo Jim behind them.

"Evening, Miss Catherine," Gumbo said, while Davy looked at him and said, "See? I told you she wouldn't go home without saying hello to us first." Their greeting made Catherine realize again that the Fox held more than the Carpenters and Mrs. Belcher.

"I'm glad your brother made it to Canada," Catherine said to Jim, "Only I'm sorry it's not easier for him there."

Jim shrugged. "Leastways, Cassius is his own man there," he said. "After I work out my time, could be I'll move up there too." With a touch of his usual wryness he added, "A couple black boys can clean chimneys up there, easy as they can in Lancaster."

Turning to Benny, Catherine reminded him that they had to get home, but Davy interrupted her. "Tell her about the eagle," he said excitedly to Jim.

"Now hush up," Jim answered with a warning glance. "That's between us two." Seeing Catherine's curiosity, how- ever, he shrugged. "Tell her, if you want to," he said, "—only, mind, it can't go no farther." He crooked his finger and beck- oned Catherine to come closer, and Davy said, "You gotta cross your heart first—but mostly you, Benny, 'cause Catherine won't blab, but this gotta be a secret." Eyes round, Benny dutifully crossed his heart and hoped to die. Satisfied, Davy cupped his hand and whispered into the ear Catherine lowered for him.

"Are you really?" Catherine asked Jim in surprise.

"Tell me too!" Benny clamored and broke into a wide smile as soon as he also got the whispered message.

"I hope you don't get into trouble for it," Catherine said to Jim. "The Squire really sets store on having that eagle chained up back here. If he finds out you let him loose, he'll make it bad for you."

"Couldn't hardly make it worse than it is already," Jim answered. "Bird like that, he got to fly free. It's something I been thinking on a long time, 'specially when he goes peck-peck-peck at his leg, where the chain is. If a rusty old chain like that gets broke, accidental like, can't blame nobody for it, way I figure."

"If you think so," Catherine said, unconvinced, before making her goodbyes and, Benny firmly in tow, hurrying up the lane and down the road.

It was dark well before they got home, but not as dark as Catherine's mood as she angrily brooded about her visit with Eleanor Johns, while the blood throbbed in her head. As it got darker, she held Benny's hand more and more tightly, ignoring his excited chatter about Davy and Gumbo's plans. Hurt and discouraged, Benny gradually stopped talking and dragged behind her sulkily.

Finally, he lagged so badly that Catherine tugged his hand impatiently. "Ouch!" Benny cried. "You hurt me! How come you're mad at me, anyhow, Katlie?" he asked, tears in his voice.

Stopping in her tracks, Catherine dropped to her knees and gave him a hug. "Oh, Benny," she explained, "I'm not mad at you at all."

"You're sure acting like you are," he said resentfully. "If you're mad at somebody else, it ain't right you're taking it out on me, yet."

Catherine felt his rebuke, knowing better than he did how much she deserved it. She finally coaxed him into forgiving her,

160

and the two went on, huddling closer and closer till the light from the kitchen appeared, and they saw their father silhouetted in the door, watching for them.

That night Catherine couldn't sleep and turned from one position to another in a futile attempt to ignore the corn husks poking her through the mattress ticking. Try as she would to stop thinking, her mind insisted on racing back through the afternoon, till she finally fell asleep. When she woke in the morning, Catherine's first thought wasn't a thought at all, but an image of Eleanor Johns staring at her in the grey dawn.

At breakfast when Gideon asked her about her visit to the Fox, she answered evasively and was relieved when Benny broke in to describe in exaggerated detail their encounter with the turkey buzzards, though he didn't say a word about the eagle. To her discomfort, Gideon came back to the subject after patiently listening to his son. "Did Mrs. Johns want anything in particular?" her father asked, his experience of the Carpenters suggesting that their social gestures usually had a motive.

"In a way," Catherine answered slowly. "There was something she thought maybe I could do for her. I said I'd think about it."

Gideon raised an eyebrow. "Oh?" was all he said before he turned his attention back to the scrapple and molasses on his plate.

Getting up to clear the empty platter and fetch the pie her father expected to finish his breakfast with, Catherine brushed against a fork, which bounced off a chair and clattered onto the floor, to the delight of Benny and Paul. "Katlie's *dopplich!*" Paul said in high glee, and Benny said, "We're going to get company, ain't so, Pap?"

"Could be," Gideon answered, wiping molasses from his plate with a slice of bread. "You and Katlie missed what we got yesterday."

"Who was it, Pap?" Catherine asked. Instead of answering in his recent clipped way, Gideon replied that it was someone who really came to see Catherine but used the excuse of business with her father, badly as shyness went with red hair.

"Did Jake stop in again?" Catherine asked in surprise.

Gideon explained that Jake was on his way back from delivering his load at Columbia. "He said he'd been thinking over how the field by the quarry got measured and had an idea it might of been done wrong," Gideon said, adding that he'd asked Jake to visit again when he had time and try out his idea. "So," Gideon concluded, "could be the fork means Jake's coming again. Or could be John Skiles wants to check up on us."

"Did you ask him to stay for supper?" Catherine asked.

"Nope," Gideon answered studying her over his bread. "Seemed to me John Skiles would eat up everything in sight, and we'd all go to bed with our bellies empty."

The boys giggled, but, in no mood for teasing, Catherine dished out the pie in silence. As he took his hat from the peg and started for the door, the boys at his heels, Gideon paused. "I did tell Jake to stay for supper," he said.

21.

As out of sorts as Catherine was, everything went wrong for the rest of the day, from the curd, which crumbled when she tried to cut it and slipped into the whey, to the bread, which perversely refused to rise. Even the cows noticed her mood when she carried her buckets to the barn for afternoon milking.

By now three of them had come in fresh, the newest calf born only the day before. When Catherine went into the pen, it started to its feet and, moving as if it didn't know yet that its legs would bend, bucked and plunged its way through the bedding to huddle behind its mother, who lowed at Catherine defiantly.

When Catherine finally managed to get cow and bucket in position, the cow looked at her accusingly and refused to let down her milk, as though she knew that Gideon was going to sell her calf when it was weaned. After several tries, Catherine moved on to the other cows, growing calmer with the steady pull of the teats. When she went back to the first one, it let her move aside the calf and get on with the milking.

The boys were off on an afternoon ramble, and Gideon was at the other end of the stable currying the horses, but he left them and came over to Catherine, curious to find out what, specifically, Eleanor Johns had wanted.

Keeping her face half buried in the shaggy coat of the cow, Catherine described her visit and didn't raise her eyes to Gideon, who leaned against the partition, listening. Speaking in brief, rhythmic phrases, she explained Eleanor Johns' condition and the plans for a secret birth.

She finished stripping off the cow and stood up. "The upshot is," she declared, "Eleanor wants me to take the baby and raise it for her. That way she can keep on being a fine lady, and I can carry her shame." As though a dam had burst, Catherine's anger rushed out, in her relief at finally telling someone, and she denounced one member after another of the Carpenter family, including Miss Sophia Passmore and throwing in Mrs. Belcher for good measure. "Why would I do a thing for any of them?" she concluded, "—when if it hadn't been for the Squire, Mama wouldn't have died!"

"That will do, Katlie!" her father ordered, angry in turn. "I never want to hear that kind of talk from you again. The Lord saw fit to take your mama," he continued, as if he were repeating a lesson he'd learned by heart. "She was worn out from the fever last summer, and she wasn't strong enough for the extra burden." He paused, making sure Catherine absorbed every word. "Your mama was going to die anyway," he said, "and I won't have you blaming anybody for what was the Lord's will." He turned his back and started towards the door.

"But Pap," Catherine called after him, "what am I supposed to do about Eleanor?"

Without turning around, Gideon called back, "Do what you want. Whatever you decide, it's between you and your own conscience."

Catherine stared after him, while the cow lowed behind her. She was just in time to stop her from kicking over the milk bucket.

In spite of the dropped fork, no visitor showed up at the Landises that day or through the weekend. Although she'd been invited to a frolic, Catherine stayed home Saturday and carded wool for summer spinning. Palm Sunday was also lonely, falling on an alternate week when the Reformed Mennonites were taking their turn at the Stumptown meetinghouse.

Monday dawned grey and overcast, though it cleared enough by afternoon that Catherine could no longer postpone her garden work, especially because the perennials were badly in need of pruning, their straggling condition a clear indication of how ill Elizabeth had been through the fall, when she should have readied them for spring.

Catherine was halfway down a row of raspberries by the far fence, when someone hailed her. Looking around, she saw a tiny figure in a green bonnet just outside the gate. Reluctantly, Catherine got up from her work and went to meet Eleanor's aunt, Miss Sophia Passmore.

"I've caught you gardening," the lady said pleasantly. "I have one myself, but I'm away so much that I pay a neighbor to look after it for me." Peering past Catherine into the garden, she added, "My, but yours looks neat and well kept. Is that a rose bush where the paths cross?"

Catherine nodded but refused to take Miss Passmore's hint. The garden got shown to friends and relatives, but she had no intention of welcoming Sophia Passmore into it. To forestall more pleasantries, Catherine said, "You came to ask me if I'll take Eleanor's baby, ain't?"

"And to tell you that Eleanor and I are leaving next Tuesday for Bedford Springs," Miss Passmore answered. "I have to know your answer before we leave. Have you thought it over?"

"I can't see my way to it," Catherine declared resentfully. "The Squire did enough to hurt my family, that I'm the last person you should ask to clean up his messes."

While she answered, Miss Passmore raised her eyebrows and drew her eyes wide. "Oh, my dear!" she exclaimed. "You don't understand. This has nothing to do with my brother-in-law! It's been my own idea, from first to last, for Eleanor's sake—and surely, you can't judge her by her father. Eleanor doesn't know about anything he may have done."

Disarmed by Miss Passmore's confession and feeling the justice of her words, Catherine answered stubbornly, "If Eleanor got herself into trouble, she should be ready to take the consequences," adding, "She's a grown-up, and old enough to know right from wrong."

Sticking to her argument like a burr, Miss Passmore instantly responded, "Eleanor is only a child. I've done the best I could by her, but both of us know she's as flighty as a butterfly—and has just about as much sense of right and wrong. Oh, no, my dear," she concluded, shaking her head, "you can't hold Eleanor to ordinary standards, because she hasn't any sense of them."

Uncomfortably, Catherine realized that Miss Passmore's straightforward evaluation agreed all too well with her own. Worse, it reminded her of the protectiveness she'd felt towards Eleanor while she sat in the kitchen at the Fox.

Eleanor's aunt continued to talk, half as though she were thinking out loud but aiming every word at her companion, whom she glanced at now and then to make sure she was listening.

"It's not as though Eleanor doesn't have good qualities," she said pensively. "Her father spoiled her so badly that, of course, she's thoughtless, but she was an affectionate child, and that hasn't changed—even when she's put her trust in the wrong places."

Catherine glanced at her suspiciously, wondering if the last comment was aimed at her. The older woman, however, gazed at the rose bush and continued her monologue. "And the best of Eleanor's affection is on this baby. She might be different if she hadn't lost the first one, you know, and now she has to give this one up," she concluded, slowing her words for emphasis.

Catherine couldn't restrain her incredulous look. "Of course, she doesn't want to," Miss Passmore countered, "but we've told her there's no other way. It wasn't easy, but I finally convinced her—but only," she added, "if I can promise that the child will be raised by someone she trusts."

Catherine remembered Eleanor visiting with her and asking all about Catherine's little brothers, or else falling into one of her reveries. "I'm sorry for Eleanor, I really am," she said sincerely. "Only, I still don't see why you're asking me."

Miss Passmore smiled wanly. "The simple truth is, you're the only person she'll give the baby up to," she said, adding quickly that the Squire would pay handsomely as long as the child stayed with Catherine.

The figure she named was so big that Catherine's eyes widened in surprise. She turned away and stared towards the new house before trusting herself to answer. "I can't say the money wouldn't be a help," she said slowly, "or that we couldn't use it. But if I did decide to do it, it would have to be for Eleanor and because I thought it was right."

Sophia Passmore searched her face. "You're Eleanor's only chance now," she said. Abruptly, she raised her neatly gloved hand and, with a brief farewell, walked towards the lane. A few steps away she turned and added, "Remember, we leave tomorrow a week."

Angered as she was by it, Sophia Passmore's visit left Catherine much to brood over. Although she knew that the meddling old lady was trying to manipulate her, still, much of what she'd said was too true to ignore. Eleanor didn't have any sense of responsibility, and Catherine knew it was wrong to judge the daughter by what the father had done.

The more she thought about it, the more tangled the problem became, till she started to wonder what her life would be like if, indeed, she did agree to take Eleanor's child. As her father had said, her decision was between her and her own conscience, but her conscience was badly muddled just now, and she became more and more lonely for her mother, wondering what Elizabeth would have wanted her to do.

While she was making Wednesday dinner, it came to her that

she should take a loaf of bread to Lena Groff, who was known to make quiet grumblings about her daughter-in-law's baking. Elizabeth had liked to stop by for a chat with the old woman, and, besides, Catherine was especially grateful for her kindness when her mother died. Elizabeth would be pleased if she looked in on Mrs. Groff.

Accordingly, dishes washed up, Catherine packed a basket with a loaf of fresh bread, a small crock of apple butter, and a vanilla pie to satisfy Mrs. Groff's sweet tooth.

The Groffs lived farther down the road, not far from where the road the Landises lived on intersected with one through West Enterprise, though, like most plantations, it was screened from the road by trees and only visible from halfway down the lane. The house was a proper one of brick, not as big as the one Gideon planned, but substantial and built against the small original structure, where Mrs. Groff had separate quarters and could escape from her daughter-in-law.

Nevertheless, the barn and outbuildings were less impressive than Gideon's, just as Dan Groff was known to be a less successful farmer. But old Mrs. Groff's garden was a model of neatness. Even this early, it was flourishing, and Catherine wasn't surprised to see Lena Groff's broad backside in the farthest quadrant, where, carefully transplanting some herbs, she looked as though she were praying in the open air.

As Catherine approached, the Groff's dog started barking and yapping, setting the poultry off in a miscellaneous chorus of squawks and quacks, with high-pitched giggles from the guineas. Only the peacock continued his jerking strut in superior unconcern, as Catherine slipped through the gate and into Lena Groff's garden.

Once inside, she hesitated, not knowing if the old woman knew she was there. But though she hadn't looked around, Mrs. Groff called a greeting, adding, "Chust let me finish this, onct."

Catherine made her way down a path banked with boards against the raised soil and past the Adam and Eve plant to where Mrs. Groff was working. A brisk order warned her to stop there.

"I won't have anybody tramping down the ground onct it's readied," she explained, carefully smoothing soil around a root. "There now," she said, struggling to her feet. "Garden work don't get no easier on the knees at my age, but, ach, what can you do, when nobody else in the house is fit to do it?"

Catherine stretched out a hand to help steady her as she picked her way down a board and stepped into the path. She broke into a smile when she saw Catherine's basket. "We'll go in the house awhile," she announced. "Peaked as you look, you could do with a cup of sassafras tea."

Catherine hated sassafras tea, but she followed obediently, soothed by Mrs. Groff's comfortable chatter about what she was planting and which sign of the moon was right for each. "It's not like many young people pay much mind to important things nowadays," Mrs. Groff remarked, as she led the way to her kitchen, a room much like the one the Landises lived in.

While Mrs. Groff bustled about the fireplace, Catherine set her basket on the table and noticed another basket beside the hearth with a three-colored cat inside, nursing kittens.

"I know I shouldn't have her in the house," Mrs. Groff explained defensively, "but this is her second litter this year. Last time the tommy killed every last one of them. So when I found this batch in the brooder house, I just picked them up and brought them in here with me. It ain't right she has to lose all her babies, yet.

"Besides," Mrs. Groff added, "their mam's a real good mouser. Can you use any more barn cats over home? That one's going to be wonderful pretty."

Pausing beside Catherine, she pointed to a little grey one, which mewed sharply when she picked it up and thrust it into her guest's hands but quieted when Catherine held him against her breast. "Chust look at that," Mrs. Groff remarked cheerfully. "He can't even see yet, and he's taken to you already. Best give him back to his mam now," she added, "or he'll get sore eyes."

Catherine put the kitten back in the basket and helped get the tea ready, while Mrs. Groff chatted about the weather and her favorite granddaughter, who, she explained, didn't take one bit after her mother. Her eyes crinkled with pleasure when Catherine unpacked her basket, and she insisted on cutting each of them a slice of Catherine's bread and fetching some smearcase to go with the apple butter. Sitting at the table with her, Catherine felt more at home than she had since her mother died and dawdled over her tea, partly to prolong her visit and partly to avoid a second cup.

Finally, she heard herself asking, "Mrs. Groff, did anyone ever ask you to do something really hard?—when they didn't have the right and they're awful people, yet?"

Mrs. Groff offered Catherine more tea and poured another cup for herself before she answered. "Folks are always coming to me and asking will I pow-wow for them," she finally said, "though it wonders me sometimes how they got the nerve." She dropped her voice confidentially. "A couple years back a certain party come by, and he asked me would I pow-wow for his baby. It was opthima—peensie, you know—and not in a way to live. And all the while I knew clear as you're sitting here that he was the one that raided Daniel's smokehouse and cleaned out every bit of meat from fall butchering!"

"How'd you know who did it?" Catherine interrupted curiously.

"Well," Mrs. Groff retorted, "I chust said to Dan, 'Now, don't let on what happened, and don't tell none of the neighbors.' And sure enough, a couple weeks later this fellow—mind, I'm not naming names—asks Dan did he find out who robbed the smokehouse yet?" She beamed at Catherine and waited for her nod before going on with her story.

"Now, I don't know that he even knew that we knew, but we did, all right, especially after a whole winter of dried beans and sauerkraut," she said indignantly. She leaned forward until her breasts rested on her folded arms. "And that's the man had the gall to come here and ask me to help him!"

"What did you do?" Catherine asked.

Mrs. Groff sat back in her chair, her face suddenly mild. "I told him I'd think on it," she said simply. She was silent, while Catherine waited expectantly. "It took me close to a week," Mrs. Groff resumed, "but bit by bit it come to me that no matter what I thought about the father, or the mother either—and she wasn't no better than she should of been—I had to try for that little baby. After all, he couldn't help who his pap was."

Catherine's eyes were wide as she asked if Mrs. Groff saved the baby.

"Well, no," Mrs. Groff answered. "He died anyhow. Only I tried the hardest I could and, mind, I never can tell if it will do any good."

Catherine's spirits sank as she thought of Eleanor Johns and wondered if she should do what Miss Passmore wanted. She was staring dismally into her teacup, when Mrs. Groff added to her story.

"Now, mind, that was chust the baby I helped," she explained. "Later on that same party come by again, yet. This time he had the wildfire and asked me would I pow-wow for him." Catherine looked up from the cup. "I chust said, I wouldn't dream of it," Mrs. Groff declared, "and I asked him didn't he maybe have something on his conscience that needed cleared before he come running to me for help. After all," she said, "people got to take responsibility for what they do—and he wasn't the one ate beans and sauerkraut all winter!"

Catherine sighed and got up from the table, announcing that she had to get home and thanking Mrs. Groff for the tea. The old woman looked at her kindly. "Now, don't you forget to ask your pap about that kitten," she admonished. "He's sure to be a wonderful good mouser."

22.

For the next few days Catherine worked in the garden and tried to resolve the problem of Eleanor Johns. By Friday the garden looked so tidy that Gideon made a point of complimenting her on it. On Saturday Jake Good came on his promised visit.

Catherine saw him arrive and watched from the side of the kitchen window as Gideon greeted him and led Jake's horse into the barn. Jake seemed to have brought along equipment of some sort, which Gideon was helping him carry when they came out again a few minutes later. Deep in conversation, they disappeared shortly in the direction of the field by the quarry, the boys scampering ahead and disappearing in front of them.

Strangely agitated, Catherine bustled about the kitchen, thinking of how to make the old hen stewing in the fireplace fancy enough for company, but when she started to mix dough for pot pie, she spilled the flour, the dough stuck to the board, and the diamonds she finally cut it into were woefully uneven. By the time she heard the men stamping their feet and scraping their shoes outside the door an hour or so later, she wished there were no such person as Jake Good.

"We got company, Katlie," her father announced, as Catherine pretended to be surprised (though, clearly, she'd set an extra place at the table). As excited as the men's voices had been when they approached the house, the cat seemed to have got Jake's tongue the minute he stepped into the kitchen, and his earlobes turned beet red.

While they and the boys washed up, Catherine set out the pot pie, which almost disappeared among all the sweets and preserves with which she'd already loaded the table.

Jake ate hungrily, raising his eyes to Catherine's now and then and mumbling how good it was, but Catherine had to wait till they started the pie to find out what Jake and her father had been up to.

"Jake brought some news, Katlie," her father finally said. "It looks like maybe the quarry should still belong to us after all." Catherine looked from one to the other in surprise. "When he saw the field the other week," Gideon went on, "Jake got it into his head that even with the new property line, what got measured looked to be more than six chains long."

Catherine shook her head. "It was measured and written down," she objected. "We saw the papers."

Jake was too excited not to break in. "The measuring was accurate," he explained, "only it looks to me like the Squire's men used the wrong measure. They went by the engineer's chain instead of the surveyor's, and that makes a thirty-four foot difference. Till you add it all up, you got a difference of two hundred feet less than the Squire claims."

The boys had been quiet because of the company, but now they were all ears. "Is the quarry ours again?" asked Paul, while Benny looked confused. "It used to be ours and then it was the Squire's, and now it's ours again," he said to his plate, frowning.

"Well, mostly, it is," Jake said to Paul, while he aimed his words at Catherine, "all but a little piece on the far end that nobody can even get into without the rest—or by law it should be, anyhow."

As confused as Benny, Catherine looked from Jake to her father. "I don't understand," she said. "Do you mean to say we're getting the quarry back?"

Jake looked at the older man, but Gideon took another bite of pie before he answered. "I want you to understand just how it stands, Katlie—you too, Paul and Benny. In the eyes of God and justice," he continued slowly, "the quarry belongs to us and always has. Only Jake and I talked it over, and I'd have to hire a lawyer and fight the Squire to get the law to say so."

Catherine's eyes sparkled with excitement. "We finally have a chance to put that man in his place!" she exclaimed, itching for a fight and, especially, the chance to expose Will Carpenter. "Will it cost much?" she asked excitedly.

Jake resolutely studied his plate, and Gideon put down his fork. "Katlie, Katlie," he said sadly. "You know better than to think I'd go to law against any man. It don't matter for right or for wrong, because either way, I can't do it."

To prevent objections and punctuate the finality of what he'd said, he pushed himself back from the table. "And that's that," he said. "I have work to do in the barn. Come along, boys."

"I want to stay with Jake," Benny objected, but at a look from his father, he reluctantly trailed him out the door, followed by Paul.

Stunned, Catherine watched them disappear, then got up and angrily began to clear dishes. "Church rules or not," she said, shaking her head, "I still can't believe it!"

"Your pap's a proud man," Jake mused. "Could even be that if the church believed different, he still wouldn't stoop that far and think of putting himself on a level with the likes of the Squire—even if he saw a chance of finding a lawyer not in cahoots with the Carpenters."

In spite of herself, Catherine had to acknowledge the truth of what he said. She'd started to crumb the table, lost in her thoughts, when Jake reached out and took her hand.

"Sit down here, onct," he said. Suddenly self-conscious, she dropped onto the chair beside his.

Jake's ears were bright red again, and he made two false starts before he burst out, "I need to know if you're going to marry me or not." Startled, Catherine stared at him. "You know," Jake went on eagerly, "like I asked you when I was over and saw you last."

"Jacob Good," Catherine exclaimed, "you never asked me anything of the sort, and I don't know why you're funning me now!"

Jake looked startled. "Sure I did, Katlie," he said, wrinkling his forehead. "I told you about having the money together and being ready to buy a farm. What did you think I was talking about?"

"You told me about wanting to move to Canada, and that's about as much as you did tell me," Catherine retorted. "For all I knew, you were getting ready to move up north with that cousin of yours—the pretty one with the dark hair."

"Come on, Katlie. For sure, you knew better than that. I picked you out from when I saw you at the Fox first, running in and out of the kitchen with that little mustache of sweat. It sure was cute," he added. Catherine swelled with indignation, then noticed Jake's grin. "I told you before that you're pretty when your dander's up," Jake added. "What do you say, Katlie? We'll get married, ain't?"

Catherine shook her head. "I can't, Jake," she said simply.

"But how come?" Jake asked in surprise. "Your pap likes me, and I thought you did too. I really did, Katlie—or, anyways, I hoped so."

"It's not that," Catherine said, embarrassed but knowing that Jake deserved an explanation. "I can't go off to Canada or anyplace else, now Mama's gone. Somebody's got to stay with Pap and look after the boys." Giving a little shrug, she added lamely, "That's just the way it is."

Jake held onto the hand she tried to pull back. When he'd

won the tug-of-war, he leaned forward and said, "Now listen, Katlie, I'm not buying in Canada. Turns out land's as dear up there as it is here. Besides, I got things half worked out with a fellow, might let me buy in here, only it depends on if I can find the right wife."

"I don't know why you're pestering me," Catherine said, regretful and half angry that Jake was trying to break down a resolve hard enough to come to in the first place.

Still holding her hand tight, Jake continued, "This place has good land, most of it cleared, and more that two men together could open up. There's a quarry right next to it, and it has a fancy new house started, with the old one all set for a *grossdaadi* house for the girl's pap."

As he spoke, Jake was studying her face eagerly and watched it turn as pink as his ears had been earlier. "If you don't have the nerve, Jake Good!" Catherine exclaimed, "—making a deal with Pap behind my back, as if I'm some kind of mare you're trying to buy!"

"Why not?" Jake asked. "It's a good plan, ain't, with everything all worked out? Just tell me one thing I forgot—I dare you!" He beamed and squeezed her hand triumphantly, sure that she couldn't find one flaw.

But Catherine's face clouded. "Jake," she said sadly, "there's something else you don't even know about, or anyone else except Pap, that might keep me from marrying you or anybody else." As matter-of-factly as she could, she told him about Eleanor Johns and what Sophia Passmore was asking her to do.

When he'd heard her out, Jake gave a low whistle. "I knew they had a lot of nerve, but I never thought even the Carpenters had that much gall," he commented. "What are you going to do about it?"

"I'm still trying to make my mind up," Catherine answered. "Mostly, I think I wouldn't take that baby for anything, only then I start thinking about Eleanor, and it seems to me I can't say no just because she's the Squire's daughter. I have to have a better reason than that. Besides, she's so kiddish. It's like

Eleanor never grew up and I should look after her."

"Maybe it's time she started looking after herself," Jake said slowly. "Nobody can spend his whole life being taken care of. Could even be Mrs. Johns wouldn't be so kiddish if she had to face up to something for a change." He added thoughtfully, "You know, Katlie, I never heard she got a divorce."

"The way it was put through, nobody did hear, except the family," Catherine answered. She opened her eyes wide and sat straight up in her chair.

"Will you just think on that?" Jake remarked. "Come on, Katlie," he said, pulling her to her feet. "Let's go out and look over the new house. We got to see how we can get it ready enough to move into by fall."

23.

Though it was only afternoon the Monday after Easter, John Skiles was sitting in his usual place at the Fox, his belly propped on his thighs and a drink in his hand. At the other end of the Windsor settee sat Tall Hen, grumpy as ever after another fight with his wife and itching for an argument.

"Yes siree," Skiles was saying between pulls from his mug. "I told you Jackson would shake things up some and set the Union on the road to democracy."

From his end of the bench, Tall Hen snorted and nearly choked on his tobacco juice. He aimed a squirt at the spittoon, wiped his mouth with his sleeve, and declared, "John Skiles, I ain't never heard such twaddle in my life. What fer kind of democracy is that, anyhow?—firin' all the people that spent their whole lives workin' for the government—like my wife's cousin's husband once removed—just so Jackson can set things up nice and soft for his special friends? Why, Adams was a better friend to the common man than Jackson is."

"A new broom should ought to sweep clean," Skiles insisted,

against his better sense. "Jackson's just taking care of what needs cleaned up, is all."

Tall Hen snorted again. "I tell you, John Skiles, that there Jackson thinks he's some kind of a king or aristocrat or something. Why, I hear tell he's even got some artist fellow lives right in the White House, just painting his picture. And the minute he gets it done, he just sits hisself down, and he paints hisself another one, yet. You can't tell me that's the way a common man ought to behave hisself when he's settin' the Union on the road to democracy!"

As luckily as not, before Skiles could think of an answer, they were interrupted by Mrs. Belcher, all but filling the kitchen door as she peered around the taproom. When she didn't see anyone else, she waddled over to them to ask if they'd seen the Squire, who'd been at the desk earlier, examining bar scores.

"How come you want him?" Skiles asked, not about to miss a chance for gossip.

Between wheezes, the cook explained that Will Carpenter wanted to be told if Catherine Landis came by. "She's with the duchess's daughter right this minute," Mrs. Belcher explained, adding tartly, "I can't say you or me ever gets invited upstairs to visit with the Royal Family — though I used to get treated better when I was just a slip of a thing. Why, a few years back I wasn't no bigger than that Landis girl, only, workin' all the time bloats you some."

John Skiles patted his belly and nodded sympathetically — but didn't offer to look for the Squire, though he did promise to pass on the message if he saw him.

The minute the cook lumbered back into the kitchen, Skiles took advantage of the break in conversation to demonstrate that, bested or not on politics, he was still the unofficial news center of Lampeter Township.

"Guess he wants her to pass word to her pap about the latest turn in that Wilson business," Skiles commented sagely, watching Tall Hen out of the corner of his eye.

As he'd calculated, Hen forgot his grievances against Andrew Jackson. "You don't mean to say the Squire's finally doin' something on settlin' that will?" his tall neighbor asked. "I thought he was going to drag that on till kingdom come."

"I just guess he still may, too," Skiles said, nodding his head as if it was hinged on a pin in his neck, "only he got nudged some a couple days back." Having sent Andrew Jackson into temporary exile, he jogged his friend's memory about the visit to the Fox a month or so ago from Miles Wilson's brother.

"You mean that eensie-peensie fellow, up from someplace down South?" Tall Hen asked, as he cut a new plug of tobacco and carefully tucked it into his cheek. "When I recollect back, he went out of here mad as a hornet," he went on, chuckling, "and that little fellow wasn't hardly no bigger than one hisself, yet."

"Well, he come back," Skiles pronounced, "and this time he brung along that brother the Squire said was lost and got him to sign all the papers legal and proper. When they come back from upstairs, the two of them was so happy, they bought free drinks for the house. Too bad you wasn't here that day," he added smugly. "It wonders me how come you missed a party like that."

He was starting to describe the visit in detail (to the exclusion of Andrew Jackson), when Will Carpenter came back after checking some matter in the stable and settled down again to tally drink scores, carefully listing names in separate columns of credit extended and credit refused.

Skiles pushed himself up from the settee and trotted over to deliver Mrs. Belcher's message, then, just as dutifully, into the kitchen to pass the Squire's answer to the cook, hoping the Squire would balance his helpfulness against the bill he'd run up in the last month.

He and his friend were sitting by the fire a few minutes later, when Catherine appeared at the door of the kitchen, paused to look around, and made her way across the room to the tapster's grate, where Will Carpenter had retreated to take stock of his supply of Madeira and Old Monongahela. Reluctantly, she looked through the grate and cleared her throat, too quietly to be heard against the clinking of bottles. When the Squire didn't notice her, she announced, "Mrs. Belcher said you wanted to see me."

Will Carpenter looked up from the corner he was working in and walked to the grate, where he frowned at her through the bars. "What do you want to see me about?" Catherine asked, her impatience to get the business over with stronger than her dislike.

"Come closer," Will Carpenter growled, glancing towards the pair at the fireplace. "Better yet, come in here." He started to open the grated door, but Catherine didn't move.

"Anything you got to say, you can tell me here," she said.

The Squire was about to bark at her to do as he said, but apparently thinking better of it, he instead leaned towards the grate. "You been to see my daughter," he said, trying to restrain his usual volume. "I want to know what you told her. Are you going to do like she asked you?"

"You mean like you and Miss Passmore put her up to asking me," Catherine answered in an even voice.

The Squire shrugged, as though any difference didn't matter. "What did you tell her?" he demanded again.

Squaring her shoulders, Catherine answered quietly, "I told her no, I won't do it."

Clearly Will Carpenter was startled. He stared at her for a moment, then said in a wheedling voice, "Maybe you haven't thought this through yet. About the money, we can talk on that and maybe sweeten up the pot some."

Not even trying to hide her contempt, Catherine looked back at him through the grate. "This isn't about money," she said, growing bolder as she spoke. "It's about what's right. And it's not right to take away Eleanor's baby and give it to me or to anybody else. It's her baby, and she wants to keep it — or she does when she's not being explained what to do. Anyway, she told me she wants to keep it. And I told her to stand up for herself and do what she wants."

Will Carpenter glared at her through the bars he was gripping, his knuckles white. "And just who do you think you are," he growled ominously, "to think you can tell me or mine what to do? You get uppity with me, young woman, and I'll see your pap run out of Lampeter."

"Seems to me you did your best to try that already," Catherine retorted, "with the way you kept my pap from getting the money that's owed him and cheated on the measures you used to steal our quarry. Only you don't own me, and you don't own my pap, and it seems to me you have a lot more to answer for than we do."

Their voices had risen, while across the room John Skiles and Tall Hen were leaning forward, not missing a word. Skiles winked at his crony. Both their heads swiveled to follow Catherine, as she turned and hurried to the door, while the Squire bellowed after her, "You and your pap haven't heard the last from me!"

Catherine's heart was beating wildly, and her temples throbbed, but she paused long enough to cast a reproachful look back at the Squire before she stumbled outside and into the fresh air. At the mounting block she paused again and leaned against it for a moment or two.

She knew the Squire too well to think for a moment that he ever made idle threats, and she wondered what more he might have in store for the Landis family. Another moment, and Catherine squared her shoulders and set off resolutely across the courtyard and away from the Fox.

About the Author

Sara Stambaugh grew up in eastern Lancaster County, Penn-sylvania. A specialist in nineteenth-century British literature, she is a professor of English at the University of Alberta, where she has taught since 1969. In addition to her novel *I Hear the Reaper's Song* (1984), she has published a critical study, *The Witch and the Goddess in the Stories of Isak Dinesen* (1988), as well as miscellaneous stories, poems and critical articles.